S0-CAG-643

WHEN COYOTE HOWLS

WHEN COYOTE HOWLS

A LAVALAND FABLE

ROBERT FRANKLIN GISH

University of New Mexico Press
Albuquerque

Library of Congress Cataloging in Publication Data
Gish, Robert.
When coyote howls: a lavaland fable / Robert Franklin Gish.
p. cm.
ISBN 0-8263-1528-3
1. Coyote (Legendary character)—Fiction.
2. Animals—Rio Grande Valley—Fiction.
I. Title.
PS3557.I79W48 1994
813'.54—dc20
94–819
CIP

First edition

ALWAYS FOR JUDY

The coyote is a long, slim, sick and sorry-looking
skeleton, with a gray wolf-skin stretched over it,
a tolerably bushy tail that forever sags down
with a despairing expression of forsakenness
and misery, a furtive and evil eye
and a long sharp face,
with slightly lifted lip
and exposed teeth.
He has a general slinking
expression all over.
The coyote is
a living, breathing
allegory of
Want.

—Mark Twain, *Roughing It*

CONTENTS

ACKNOWLEDGMENTS

Virgil Hedrick and his brother, Roscoe, have my gratitude. They made the westering, wilderness ways of Coyote a reality for me, as did Sonny Hedrick, albeit in a more urban, suave, and totally ironic way.

And I owe much to the knowledge, the commitment, and the climbing and hiking histrionics of Buzz Buzzard. He knew his namesake and other kin with a naturalist's nearness and respect—and a thespian's sense of "soaring" and "landing," of rising action and resolution. To me he seems still a human incarnation, a reversed version of the pathetic fallacy.

My life-long amigo and compadre, Kenyon Thomas, tramped across real and imagined lavalands of New Mexico with me countless times, at times leading the way, always offering support. To him and his roaming, Yamaha ways I am always thankful.

Annabeth, I hope, will always remember the short and long treks and "the light" of our expeditions to and under the volcanoes. Robin and Stuart have, in our family nature walks seen the joy of arroyo and mesa discovery in the eyes of Matt and Joe—ever inquisitive. Timothy and Georgeann cast their own romantic and radiating patina on the petroglyphs west of Albuquerque. So many familial and fleeting West Mesa and Bosque moments, though mutable and transient, fill my days and heart. To Judy I owe all for she knows the truths of my own Coyote heart.

Also, the ever-present, always-constant, solid and *firme* Coyote of Cambria California has my abiding thanks. His still and silent howls pervade my spirit with their own haunting wakenings, alarms, and comforts.

Elizabeth Hadas is all one could want in an editor and has that special knack to bring the best of alternatives into fruition. I thank her for her understanding, sensibilities, talent, and patience. I thank Diana Stetson for the courage of question along Coyote's way. And for the rare privilege of allowing me, as author, to see her see, and together to avoid the pitfalls of cliche. Tam Davis, *una buena cantadora* herself, helped me give melody and voice to Don Coyote's at times racuous but always inspiriting *canciones.* Emmy Ezzell invariably plays and shows just the right cards. Peter Moulson knows well the wisdom of "fables" and helped clear the way in saying so.

As for the traditions of indigenous Coyote literature, oral tales, epic poetry, the romance of story, and the various myths concerning the roles of the story teller, I say "*Abrazos y gracias,*" and offer my abiding allegiance. In our lives and living we are story incarnate and it is the oral tellings which tap such essence and music most. Each family, each individual, lives out their own myths. And their often ignored or neglected tales are permanent and prevailing and must be heard. Coyote tells us so.

It is, always and forever, *la familia, la familia,* which gives meaning to lonely sojourns in the lavalands and malpais of the spirit, and celebration to the community of arrival.

All these Americans up in special cities in the sky
Dumping poisons and explosives
Across Asia first,
And next North America,
A war against earth.
When it's done there'll be
   no place

A Coyote could hide.

—Gary Snyder, "The Call of the Wild"

BLACK MESA
BLACK SNAKE ROAD
MIDDLE VOLCANO
BOCA NEGRA
FOOTHILLS
N
W
E
S
LAVA LAND

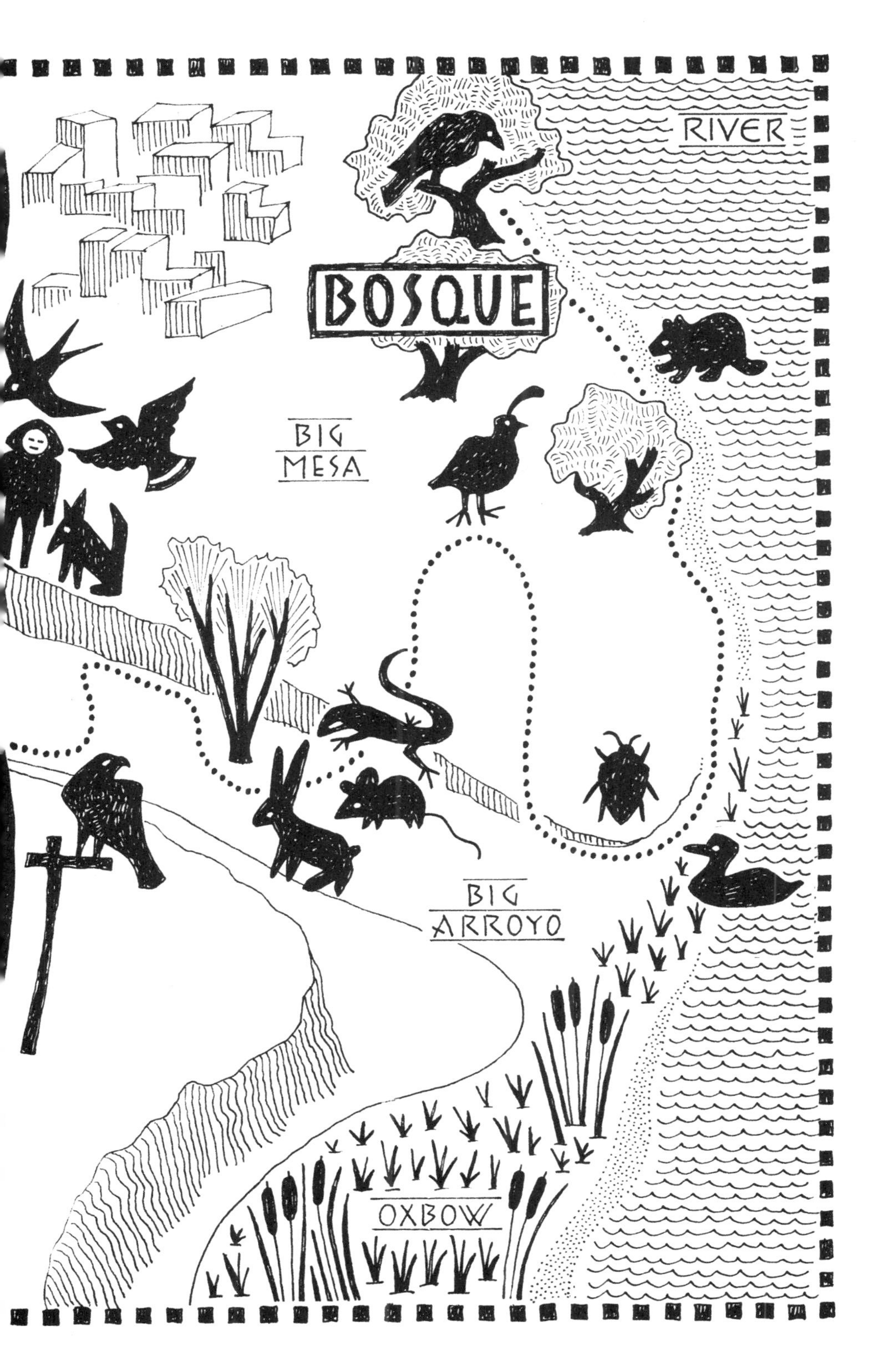
RIVER
BOSQUE
BIG MESA
BIG ARROYO
OXBOW

I saw the best minds of my generation destroyed by madness, starving hysterical
naked,

. . . .

who howled on their knees in the subway and were dragged off the roof
waving genitals and manuscripts, ...

—Alan Ginsberg, *Howl*

PREFACE

I have trailed a coyote often, going across country, perhaps to where some slant-winged scavenger hanging in the air signaled prospect of a dinner, and found his track such as a man, a very intelligent man accustomed to a hill country, and a little cautious, would make to the same point. Here a detour to avoid a stretch of too little cover, there a pause on the rim of a gully to pick the better way—and it is usually the best way—and making his point with the greatest economy of effort.

—Mary Austin, *The Land of Little Rain*

Coyote first came my way, came across my consciousness, when I was a small boy, a "chapito" out West, a "muchacho" very much in the forming. So Coyote first came to me in youth and in story. Out of reveries and a wandering, wondering mind and heart. And that's a fine coming for *ma'iitsoh,* for a slender roamer like Coyote.

Coyote first walked straight out of fertile family legend and then out of the family's desert dreams. Coyote came in the evening accounts my father would give about his twentieth-century re-enacted travels across the Llano Estacado, the plains and mesas of northern New Mexico claimed so naively yet so boldly by the Conquistadors as Nueva Granada.

My father was an explorer of another phase, part of the migration to the Southwest in the 1920s in search of a cure for tuberculosis, in search of health, of restoration. He drove a gasoline delivery truck. But the fuel he delivered to me was the stuff of story, the ignition of my boyhood imaginings, my own first spiritual westerings. And for me he was as glorious as any Conquistador. As brave and heroic as Coronado or Oñate or Cabeza de Vaca. He was for me the best of best men, *un hombre del campo, un hombre fuerte, un hombre de carne y hueso.*

"I saw a coyote today over by Moriarty," came my father's words, "and Coyote was running, running as fast as fast could be. And he was tawny-blonde and boldly big in his running. It was hot and I had the windows rolled down and here came this moving spot out of the distance. Way out yonder, East, coming out of the morning sun. Coming out of Oklahoma it seemed. Coming from Sandsprings and Tulsa. Coming out of the old Indian Territory?

"What in the Sam Hill? I say, and then I recognize it. Know it. Coyote. Señor Coyote saying hello, paying his disrespects, just being himself. Being wild. Being free. Being. Coyote.

"Coyote wasn't there to impress me. Didn't seem to care. Just ran across the road about fifty yards in front of me—right there, big as life, going fast. Coyote! Heading West with the morning sun. I watched him for a time. Admired him. Envied him. But you know how it is out there alone, son. Quiet. Silent. Nice.

"Sometimes, though, it gets to you, know what I mean? You want to talk. You want to talk to yourself. You want to talk to someone. Want someone to talk to you. And just then I wanted Coyote to howl. Wanted it in the worst way. Just wanted him to stop the shit out there and howl like hell to the Goddamn openness. To the wind. To the West. To New Mexico. To me.

"Because I felt like howling with him. I felt like hollering at the top of my lungs. Hollering with a hungering hurt. So I let out a coyote yelp or two of my own. *Yip Yip Yippie Ey O Cay Ote. Ooooooo, Coyote!*

"'Coyote! Coyote!' I called out and holler-howled to the son of a bitch. And I stopped right there in the middle of Highway 14 and took out the Winchester and let go a couple of rounds into the air. Just for the hell of it. Trying to say my own hellos, you know. Nothing much changed his running. Coyote! Then I really tried to get the old bastard's attention. I bore down on him and let go a couple of speeding bullets. *Toma. Toma. Toma, tu madre.*

"And the dirt kicked up behind old Coyote in little clouds. *El viejo! El joven!* He paused for a time. Turned around and looked back—at the truck, at me and the old .30-.30 thunder stick. Got his attention, it did. Funny thing. Didn't scare him at all, though. Boy, he was pretty. Old coyote. Young coyote. Running out there on the Moriarty mesa. Heading West out Estancia way, you know. Coyote."

And I would sit there, son to the story and the storyteller, spellbound, feeling the warmth of the ascending sun on the mesa, on the cab of the truck, picturing it all, listening to the words, to the storied sounds of my cowboy, trucking father yodeling the hell to the winds and to some kindred spirit, some urge and need and hunger of his own. In the yelling, and in the telling. And in my own listening hunger to hear and to know I was out there . . . listening to the explosion of the gun, listening for Coyote to howl, hearing it, and hearing the texture and the timbre of my father's voice and the scratchy spectacle of how there at the supper table he would pull his fingers down along his cheek and around his chin, scraping his stubble of dark, virile whiskers. Listening to him laugh. Hearing him slurp his coffee, Okie-Cherokee style, out of his saucer where he would always pour it from his steaming cup, waiting for it to cool for a minute between words and hard-fought breaths. Watching my father watch my mother out of his road weariness. Watching him look at me with an expression of love and longing for his own youth. Waiting for a wink or a smile or a rough-handed pat. There was something of old Coyote, I sensed, in my father. Especially out there on his westering route, out Moriarty way, out Estancia way, out Corona way. Journeying toward Gran Quivira. Out New Mexico way! Saying in his own way, like Coyote, like Oñate, *"Pasó por aquí."*

My father would tell of setting the throttle . . . , then he would open the door of the big green beetle of a truck and stand on the running boards yelling to the winds, thankful that his tuberculosis was on the mend in the clean wind-swept mesas of New Mexico. He could holler. He could howl. He could howl. He was alive. He was looking and listening and living. Out West. Out Coyote way.

I loved hearing my father tell about Coyote. I liked Coyote. Wasn't really afraid of him either in those storied, fanciful times. Sure, coyote was a rounder and a bounder. Stayed out late at night. Nice work if you could get it, in a boy's blossoming imaginings. And those were the words my father sang, part of his mesa music. "I'm come here to tell you boys, I'm ragged but I'm right." That was coyote. That was my father. Ragged but right. That was me in my imaginings.

Then, later, when still a growing boy, maybe eleven or twelve, one evening at twilight, while deer hunting in the Gila Wilderness in southwestern New Mexico, I heard Coyote howl. It sent shivers of wonder down my spine and awakened rememberings and recognitions of I knew not exactly what. I knew only a familiarity of some strange kind, and a strange fearful attraction. Coyote calling me.

I sought out the spot, mesmerized somehow, where I had heard Coyote howl. And it turned out to be a den of pups. They were barking. And the mother was standing there . . . listening, on top of a large mounded hill, a very special, almost sacred spot it seemed to my young heart. Then, there in the scrub-cedar shadows and in her own prominence, she looked straight at me for one of those eternal moments before she turned her head into the advancing night and she howled . . . Ooooooooooo! Coyote howled!

In some special way my connection with nature and my perceptions of it changed for all time. Was nature good in its badness? Was bad really good? Coyote in that special howling brought into question, though then not in any verbal, conscious sense, the importance of seeing beyond stereotype, of reperceiving the perceived "reality."

Most people are conditioned to either dismiss or despise or destroy coyotes. Take a poll and coyote ratings would come in low. Consider the language, the images associated with coyotes in contemporary public opinion. Pop culture would have us relegate coyotes to the anthropomorphic comedies and animated antics of Wily Coyote and Roadrunner cartoons. Is Coyote more than a pink or green or red saw-cut silhouette, bedecked with a bandanna and sold for fifty bucks to decorate some living room corner? Sure. Coyote is more than kitsch and curio.

Coyote is omnipresent, immortal, many faceted, thick and full and outside time. Transcendent in the world of myth and story. And he invites and merits our own New West reperceiving of him in all his Coyote complexity. I saw. I comprehended Coyote's spirit there in the Gila confronting Coyote face to face. If there's a rapscallion Coyote, there's a romantic Coyote too, a lingering "allegory of Want," as Twain says. Why reduce Coyote to stupid desert chase scenes and the misadventures of endless miscalculations and mistakes, victimized, foiled and flattened by first one, then another repetitious "beep beep"?

Animation isn't the culprit. Anthropomorphic portrayals *per se* are not the issue. It's all in the perceptions. The renderings. The biases, beliefs, and assumptions. Coyote occupies a chameleon, changeling place of god and devil, good and evil (though those concepts don't quite get at it), in indigenous pictured and storied portrayals of him. Why identify Coyote by names like varmint? "Varmint?" Yes and no. What's behind the bestiaries and animal hierarchies that humanity structures and applies? Coyotes are lesser animals than lions? Than bears? Than antelope or deer or elk? Than sheep and cattle? Than domesticated, capitalized, raise-to-slaughter livestock? Coyotes are lesser animals than their "prey"?

What's this "king of the beast," serpent-to-saint ranking anyway? Who's to say? What's to say? That Gila howling was, for me, although naive and unspoken in a boy's way, a kind of ecological epiphany, heard and seen and felt—communicated in Coyote's heard howl and the chorus of resonating, paternal, storied, hollering echoes. My father talked to the animals too. Hollered at Coyote. Called hogs! Well, there's a bit of the poet in all of us Coyote kin.

For many ranchers in the West, admittedly, coyotes pose a problem—as do all "predators." Stories of the Old West, not to be confused with American Indian mythology, see to it that Coyote is demonized. For urban and suburban citizens of the New West, the "new" coyote carries with him much remnant stigmatization and stereotyping as hunkering, shifty-eyed, tongue-dangling predator. People fear Coyote now more for their house cat's safety than for other nuisance or noise. What is Coyote telling us in his coming and in his staying? What's in such a word, such assumptions: *predator?*

To some minds, analogously, there is and has always

been an "Indian problem." Eradicate the Indian. Eradicate Coyote. Coyote the predator. Coyote the problem. Coyote the killer. Coyote the clown. Coyote the one. Coyote the other. But what, who is the real Coyote? And in whose perception?

The real, romantic, and reductive dangers reside not so much in attempting to empathize with Coyote but in the attitudes and assumptions which underlie the empathizing. When it comes to indigenous myths, oral tales and legends, the question of the appropriateness of anthropomorphizing Coyote is moot.

Coyote exists and has existed outside of such issues in that Coyote has been personified for ages, fulfilling the projected versions of countless personae. He is part of the eternal human quest, the human hunger to understand animals and nature. Such a quest is at once profound and problematic, answerable much better, in all probability, through narrative than exposition.

Why the need to personify Coyote? That is the question. Whether humanity will best come to know Coyote, to know animals scientifically or metaphorically or through combinations of both methods of "knowing" remains as persistent and prevailing an enigma as human nature itself.

What I know, in my individual reckoning, is that now all these years later I still hear Coyote's real and storied howl echoing through the years, reverberating around the roadways of my spirit. And now, when I sit out on my brick-floored veranda staring into the distant night with its mysteries of dark and light, I listen with the keenest attention to the coyotes barking and yelping, yipping and howling on the mesas around the river valley, along the Rio Grande near where I was born. The place I call home.

I read many meanings into that mesa music. Meanings for Coyote and for me and for human beings and for wilderness and its myriad majestic calls of celebration and warning. Just what happens to Coyote, to his kin and his prey, and to the human spirit when Coyote howls is impossible to explain or describe. Just who Coyote is and what he really represents is a mystery. Coyote adapts. Coyote endures.

What is essential, however, is that Coyote continue to howl, to be left alone and allowed to howl his own special Coyote courage and constancy. And for us, his human cousins, what matters is that we continue to listen to Coyote—and our own urges, our own wild and cunning compulsions against modernity and madness, our own needs to howl. Courageous Coyote. Creative Coyote. Constant and continuing Coyote.

What follows is an imagined and artificial, albeit authentic howling of my own. A tale of Lavaland. A myth of the modern West in all its ambivalence and change, all its cultural and regional angst. Yes, it's an anxious place, the West. Always has been. It's violent and angry and still stirring and seeking, still ever hungry, turning back to reexamine its earlier selves and shadows.

So here's to Coyote! Here is a testimonial holler and "howl," and a wish that the developing myth of the best West, the at once renewed and New West, might be so.

Perhaps it is a story you have heard. A story you are hearing in your daily struggles, hopes and dreams. Perhaps it is one you will want to tell. For Coyote comes to all of us, out of story, out of dream, out of ourselves.

If I were to attach my own personal interpretations to this particular version of the Coyote mythos, I would link it to the writer's hunger for an understanding of and an ability somehow to express and partake of the workings of the creative imagination and of fancy.

A craving, in my mind, not unlike the urges of *Canis latrans* to sing, to speak, to howl, and a process of poetizing much belabored by the Romantic poets, especially in their attempts not only to find a voice but to keep it. "A timely utterance gave that thought relief, / And I again am strong." So says Wordsworth of his own "intimations." They are not unlike Coyote's. Coyote the singer. Coyote the teller. Coyote the utterer.

It is no coincidence that story and Coyote are companions. For Coyote is, among other things, at least for those of us in the West, the embodiment of the creative imagination.

When Coyote Howls is the first in a series of narratives about the volcanic malpais country of New Mexico, most particularly the various volcanoes of the Rio Grande Valley around Albuquerque, Isleta, Los Lunas, Jemez, Los Alamos, Santa Fe, and Taos. Although Coyote exists outside of time, most of these myths of the modern West that make up the Lavaland Tales will be set in the second half of the twentieth century. The volcanoes of the American West, of New Mexico and their accompanying "badlands," or *malpais,* as the early Spanish colonizers called them, are spectacular in their landscapes and legends—and provide the fervent makings of many geological as well as historical and literary plottings.

The lavalands of this legendary telling are classified by scientists as Monogenetic volcano fields. It is an awesome, sublime field—literally and figuratively. The language of such descriptions rings with its own scientific mysteries, as offered by A. M. Kudo (*Volcanoes of North America,* p. 302):

> The three earliest flows [of the Albuquerque volcanics] cover an area of 60 km^2 and are eroded on the eastern edge, forming what is locally called the 'Volcano Cliffs,' which have a large concentration of petroglyph art. Later flows are more restricted and localized. Most of the cones have cinders, but considerable amounts of lava and spatter are found even on the summits. The highest cone (Vulcan or J Cone) [*sic*] is in the southern alignment -55 m above the highest lava flows. The base of this cone has a thick unit of cinders, but toward the top a lava dome formed which has been split subsequently into north-south halves by an explosion crater which has only remnant east and west rims. Semi-radial dikes and dribble flows cut the dome.
>
> Slight differentiation has been detected in the basalt. The older flows have olvine and plagioclase phenocrysts in a matrix of plagioclase, augite, opaqueness, and glass. Pigeonite occurs in the groundmass in the youngest rocks. All flows are hypersthene normative.

Names and identities of the five volcanoes on Albuquerque's West Mesa vary. Spanish and Anglicized names prevail, evidence of the near-sighted ethnocentrism of the "young" West. Older yet still abiding

American Indian names for these sacred places remain obscure, known only to the initiated. But the sublimity of these landforms resides outside any naming.

When Coyote Howls attempts to tell of Lavaland more in the language of legend than of science. Both accounts, both "stories" offer only glimpses of some sublime shadows of the magnitudes these lavalands hold. Which is to say, this is only one lavaland tale, set in a land of many such spectacles, many such enchantments. And in such lands as this is Coyote. Coyote is in these lands. Coyotlinauatl, Tezcatlipoca, Huehuecoyotl, Coyotl, the Aztecs called him. Ma'iists o'si, say the Navajo.

His other names are legion. In all his forms, living up to all his names, Coyote is in these lands. And Coyote is coming along . . . . To him I say, "Siyo" and "Tadaya'i Estat D'Guni."

Ándale, ándale pues. . . . Coyote comes. Coyote comes.

CHAPTER ONE

They are not happy with the way things are. They know what a bad time it is. They can tell by the moon when the world is cockeyed . . . . They understand the signs. This earth is cockeyed.

—James Welch, *Winter in the Blood*

But for the larger mammals the question of how to live in the desert tends to become unanswerable when the desert is inhabited by man.

—Joseph Wood Krutch, *The Voice of the Desert*

Raven was restless in his river roost. Moon had an ashen cast and a bit of a blurred ring. Raven turned his head to look up. And down. And around. He bobbed and ducked and teetered back and forth. He blinked his onyx eyes. And blinked again. And yet again. His mouth was open and salmon pink, the air cold in the breathing. He cawed softly. Croaking. Repeatedly. Almost clucking.

"CAWWW, CAWWW, CAW."

His raven brother answered in response. "CAWW, CAW." There was small comfort in such common calling. Raven's thoughts were disturbed. Raven was bothered by the sounds of another kind and kin.

Raven jumped from one branch to another, balancing with his large extended wings, and then back again. The wind ruffled his soft feathers and when it blew against them it penetrated deep to the skin. Even his long, widely set scaled legs ached for more feather covering. His long clawed toes curled and uncurled around the cottonwood branch. All night he had looked at the moon with a gnawing knowledge that something was awry.

Things had been fine at yesterday's sunset. Summer was all but over and change was in the air. He had flown up the river from the valley fields as was his habit. To the east, Sandia Mountain, watermelon-pink in the sunset, had framed Raven's flight. The wind was chilly on his wings.

To the west, the shadow-fronted volcanoes and the lavalands around them had been framed by a ribboned backdrop of sun declining into an evening glow after a particularly brilliant splurge of orange and red light. The river was sluggish, its slow brown waters sparse, and the ditches were slow-moving.

Flying over the River bridge last evening had caused a slight shudder and shiver of Raven's feathers, and more than a cawing or two of sorrow. The humans seemed more frantic than usual in their own journeys home along their snaking asphalt pathways. They too felt the season's shifting. There would be more roadkill in the morning, carrion for Raven and his kin to recognize and remove. The big dirt mound by the Oxbow, where the human engineers had begun their diggings for water diversion, was littered with the bones of victims. Raven lamented such plenty. Mopping up this largesse could become too much. Death was working overtime these days, when the valley fields were full of seeds and grain awaiting harvest.

Diving into the river cottonwoods to roost last evening had climaxed a good day for Raven. But the end-of-the-day cawing and commotion had soon silenced into cold drowsiness as night descended. Raven hunkered low on his perch in an ancient and ample cottonwood. The treetop breeze was filled with the river aromas of the ripening autumn and the distant smell of piñon smoke.

Fall and its rhythms were familiar. But Moon, once she topped the mountains, was strange somehow, ringed and rimmed with cloudy signs of an early storm. The dancing lights of the city just beyond the Bosque were arcing and searching and nervous. Highway and street noises pulsated. Reverberated. Vatos and valley riders boomed and bounced along West Central, headed for the edgy and spectacular palisade sights of Patrick Hurley Park. Headed for Tingley Drive and the cool of cottonwood shadows. *Ése, a dónde va?* Carnalismo cool.

Raven's animal cousins caged in the nearby Valley

zoo emitted exotic and foreign roars and squawks. And Raven could not sleep. Things had changed. Again. Things were not settled. Again. Things were cockeyed. The evening winds whistling off Black Mesa and the volcanoes to the west told him as much.

"Moon is not right this night, that is certain, and City refuses to sleep," Raven remembered quietly chattering in the night, causing morning to come slow and hard. "I am thankful for Sun's consent to appear this day. For Night was not right. Neither in its circled lights nor in its cloudy darkness or its wind-whispering messages."

Cottonwood always listened closely to Raven. And cottonwood knew of Raven's restlessness. Raven's cottonwood roost was as recurring as the changes of river and bosque. Intimacies were established.

Rest Raven. Rest.
Rest Raven. Raven rest.
Raven. Raven. Raven.
What is wrong, Raven?
What is it, Raven? What?
Yes. Summer goes. Summer goes.
Autumn comes. Autumn comes.
Autumn comes. Autumn comes.
Ah, but Autumn comes golden.
Ah, yes. Autumn comes . . . golden!
Before the shivers of winter.
Before the cracking branches.
Before us. Before us.
Autumn comes. Autumn comes.
And, ah, Autumn comes golden.
Autumn comes golden. And, and. . .
And gold compliments you so well, Raven.

Gold compliments . . . you. So well.
Autumn comes. Golden comes Autumn.
Yes. Yes. Autumn comes.
Autumn comes golden.
And, Raven, gold compliments you so well.
Rest, Raven.
Rest. Rest. Rest.
Raven, rest. Rest.
Soon my turning leaves will fall.
With fall soon my turning leaves will fall.
But now . . . Raven. Raven.
Autumn comes golden.
Now, Raven, r e s t . . . r e s t.
Raven, r e s t, r e s t.
Autumn comes golden, comes golden.
Raven . . . , you know. You know.

Raven appreciated the whispering consolations of Cottonwood. It was why he returned. Each day. Each year. Cottonwood was always inviting his return. And Raven was keen on rhythm and routine and the goodness of the ordinary. He much preferred the usual. And so he turned on his branch and welcomed morning in his usual and accustomed way with his best, most hopeful song.

For Raven knew advancing autumns promised even earlier winters:

Come. Come. Come. Come Morning.
I send out my song to you. Yes.
I send a song of welcome. Come.
Come Morning.
Morning come walking here.
Morning come walking near.

Morning. Come awakening.
Come awakening. Morning.
Morning come awakening.
Come, come, come.
Come, come, come.
Come Morning with Sun.
Come with the Dawn.
Come with Autumn's gold.
Come with Daylight promise.
Come with Night's ending.
Come with Dream's fulfilling.
Come. Come. Come. Morning.
Come, come, come Morning. . . .
Morning come walking near.
Morning come walking here.

And then, more suddenly than he could comprehend, Raven stopped and remembered. He had dreamed last night, even in his wakefulness. A disturbing dream. A daunting dream. Yes, Dream had come his way. That is why he was restless. Uneasy. Restless even in the residual, risen morning. In his dream, Coyote had come to him for help as a brother.

Two predators who understood the need for tricks now and then, even on each other. For disdain. For hypocrisy. For survival. Coyote was bothered and needed answers and advice. He had come to Raven in the silver shadowing moonlight and he had looked up at him, silhouetted on his cottonwood branch against Moon.

Coyote had thrown back his head and howled at Raven. But. . . Raven could not make out the words. Raven could not hear Coyote's howling. It was, Raven first thought, another of Coyote's tricks. Perhaps

Coyote was just pretending to howl. But then Coyote howled again, and again, and once more, tossing his head far back, yipping, yipping, yipping. Yipping and barking, barking and yipping at Moon.

> Yippppppppp Ooooooooooo.
> Yip, yip, yip, hooowhooo.
> Yip, yip, yippy, hoooowhooo.
> Ooohooowoooooooooooooooo.
> Yip. Yip. Ooohooooooooo.

And Raven was deaf to his brother's voice. Raven was deaf. Raven must be deaf. He could not hear Coyote's howl. Coyote would not joke about such serious things. Not about this. No. Not the Coyote he knew.

"I can see when Coyote howls. But I do not hear his howl. What meaning does Dream bring me?" thought Raven. And he cawed, cawed and called out in his loudest voice, "Caw! Caw! Caw! Gaw! Gaw! Gaw!," more to hear the sound of what he was saying than the sense of it. Just to make sure that he, that Raven, the one who points the way in his seeing, could hear. Raven called out again. And once more:

> Caw. Caw. Caw. Come.
> Come. Come. Come Morning.
> Come Morning. Come.
> Come Morning. Come Morning.
> Come Morning. Near Morning.
> Come Morning. Here Morning.
> Caw. Come. Come.
> Caw. Caw. Come . . . .

And there, coming with the morning, was Coyote. Coming out of dreams to talk to Raven. Seeking out brother Raven. Coming to talk about last night's moon. Coming to talk of last night's winds. For it was Moon who, with Wind's assistance, had stolen Coyote's howl. That was the answer. Of this Coyote was convinced. And Coyote knew he had to find his howl. Had to find how to get his howl back.

Raven knew such things too. Deep down. These things he knew for certain. As certain as his caw and its cawing calling. As certain as Morning's coming. As certain as his wings. As certain as his feathers and their iridescent, sable blackness. As certain as his ruffling-soft, black-feathered breast.

Raven knew these things so well that even before Coyote arrived at River Bosque, Raven knew and was convinced of Coyote's coming . . . coming out of night turned morning, coming tawny-furred out of Dream into Dawn.

And so Raven looked down through the soon barren-branched bosque, through the leaf-rattling, golden-hued, comforting Cottonwood, to see Coyote. To see Coyote coming. To see Coyote standing, his black-ringed tail low against the grey-brown, gnarly trunk of ancient, friendly, commodious Cottonwood.

Raven blinked twice to be sure Coyote was really there and not something out of Dream's shadows. One could never tell about Coyote. Not Coyote the trickster. Coyote the chameleon. He could appear and disappear in one swish of his dark-edged tail, in one Raven blink. And he did not always come in truth. Not Coyote. Raven knew Coyote. He knew him. He was . . . almost sure. Coyote.

Coyote often came in fun and in trickery. Came in

meanness and mischief and mockery. Coyote the rapscallion. Coyote the believing. Coyote the ingenuous. Coyote the fool. Coyote, the heart's hero. Coyote the lover. Coyote the thinker, the tinkerer. Coyote the crier. Coyote the creator. Coyote the roamer. Coyote the changeling. Coyote the comer. Coyote the traveler. Coyote the goer. Like Morning, Coyote was always coming along. Coyote. Coyote. There he was. His long pointed snout raised above his white-throated neck, looking, looking up at Cottonwood. Looking up at Raven.

So Raven cautiously, but still with necessary respect, asked a question of Coyote. He was a cousin worthy of such sacred suspicions.

"Huehuecoyotl, Huehue, my Coyote *hermano,* Coyote my compadre, my companion, my bro, am I right in realizing that I did not hear your howl last night? That I was restless in the moonlight knowing you were not howling? That I felt Wind, as it rustled my night-darkened perch, carrying your howl away? Tell me, cousin, for you visited me in my dreams and I could not hear your voice. You must let me hear you howl now so that I might know I can hear and that you can howl. Raven must hear his seeing, you know."

Coyote, dream now come into dawn, reared back his head to howl. Coyote threw back his bristled neck and angular head to howl. He could not. Coyote could not . . . howl! Raven was worried at such a silent sight, seeing but not hearing when Coyote howls. And soon Coyote whimpered and spoke in a soft bark.

"Raven, Moon stole my howl last night. It was Moon. This I know. It was Moon. It was . . . it was Wind. Wind must have done Moon's bidding. It was Sun. Sun has not returned my howl. Morning gives me only the voice to whimper and whine and speak in this soft, yapping, yippy, gippy, pitiful bark. There is change in the air, across the land. You can feel it too, Raven, you of all can feel it. My parents and brothers and sisters have gone with the summer and I am now alone. Coyote. Coming alone. *Chingao! Chingao! Qué lástima!* Coyote is not meant to be so. Things are amok, my brother. Things are fucked!

"I want to howl and howl and howl. There is much urging me on to howl myself into lonely being. But I cannot howl. Try as I might, Coyote cannot howl. What am I to do? *Chingaoooo! Chingaaoooo! Shi . . . shit!"*

And Coyote's anger sputtered as he spoke to Raven. To River. And to Bosque.

"Now, Coyote," replied Raven, "this is upsetting, *Cuate,* and as serious to me as to you. Pardon me in hesitating, but you know what they say about you. *Qué Vato!* Coyote, Huehue *Hijito!* I fear you are up to no good. Fear you are fooling. Are you, in your tendencies toward mischief and misadventure, really telling me the truth? *Quiero la verdad, amigo!*

"Remember, Raven is much like you. *Con permiso, quiero decir algo . . . .* Have you cleaned out your stomach and vacated your bowels this morning? They say, and I have seen and heard it in the past, that you howl from both ends, from your mouth and your behind. I hesitate, *hermano,* to say this or offend you by calling you "Ass-barker" this chilly, Raven-rankling morning. *Esta mañana, mendigo,* I am in no mood for fooling around. It is natural and helpful for me to hear you howl, but I do not want any morning stench of your leavings here around my river roost. *Comprende, muchacho?* Have you consumed any peppers lately?

Do you have the hots, *Jovencito?* Running, *Oye,* with the runs? *Sabes?"*

"Cállete su boca! Raven, *claro que sí,* I do not greet you or the morning with insults and bad names. Please reciprocate. You are the chile eater, not me. Let's not argue about diet. You eat everything, *cabrón! Ayúdame Pájaro Negro!*

"It is a fast fall coming our way. My youth is over and I am set forth on my own. You are the one, with your keen vision into the nature of things, to help me, to show me the way. I tried to howl last night and Moon and Wind conspired to take my howl from me. This I know. Or so I suspect. This is quite a crisis for Coyote. Stressful. Anxiety causing. I'm a bundle of nerves, as they say. You have to help me convince Moon and Wind to return my howl. You will sleep better for it, *Profeta,* as will all my cousins."

"Qué joven! Tu coco no patina! Qué tonto ese buey! You jump to conclusions so easily, Coyote my boy. For a wise young fellow you lapse into fallacies of logic. Did your parents not teach you how to reason? Moon *might* have stolen your howl. And Wind often does her bidding, yes. They are familiar collaborators just as we are companion conspirators.

"Wind did whistle and whisper around me in a discomforting way in the night. But Wind has his own howl, as you know. Your assumption is possible. For, as you know, Moon is fickle in her many faces. And I am a kind of corroborative witness—of sorts. But then again Moon might not be the prime culprit at all. Just because you lost your howl after Moon appeared does not mean Moon is the cause of such misadventure and mischief.

"Cabeza de cuete! Use your native-born common

sense. Avoid such *post hoc ergo propter hoc* thinking, as my amigo Edgar would say. You are a wise and wily fellow in both life and legend. This I know. Perhaps you lost your howl yourself, *sabes.* Moon may well have seen what happened, keen observer that she is. Wind might be trying to return your howl. Give you some of his. Let us explore all possibilities. This is a time for true smarts. Are you absolutely certain that your howl is lost?"

"Raven, *espérate, por favor,* do not confuse my Mestizo heritage with an ability to speak classical Latin. Please *post* your own *ergo propter hoc.* I would not joke with you about this. *No tengo ningun chistes hoy, hombre.* Believe me. I am sincere. And, *Ése* bro, you have your dream. If you want evidence, call on Dream. Ask your friend Edgar about deduction and ratiocination. You of all my cousins should know that superstition and mystery have their own kind of logic. This is not the time to betray yourself to what you are calling 'reason.'"

"Of course, Coyote *Vagabundo. Usted tiene razón.* You are right. But the search for your lost or stolen or forgotten or neglected howl might be more difficult than you think. It might be easier than you think. You understand. Perhaps your howl is just visiting somewhere and will soon return. Perhaps what you need most to do is just practice."

"Don't try such empty consolation with me, Raven. I come to you in truth and want the same in return. These are serious times, times of large and small, personal and universal transitions, and things are not right with me. I must have my howl to cope with these changes of season and my personal stage of life. I must howl to be Coyote, to be who I am. When Coyote howls but can't be heard then things are cock-eyed. Damnit, don't you know this in all seriousness and sincerity?"

"Well, Coyote my Hispano, my Latino, my Mestizo, my Chicano, my Indio friend . . . I concede you are right. In truth I think you must do a very big thing. You will have to go on a journey in search of not just the sounds and sirens of your howl but what it really is—your very self and how others see you. How you see yourself.

"In my dream I saw another suggestion about what you must do. I fear you must travel . . . down River a distance, then along Big Arroyo, and cross Black Snake Road. Yes, Black Snake Road! This is a most dangerous crossing, *amigo.* Then you must travel beyond the snaking highway and cross Foothills, and climb Malpais to Black Mesa and the fingered tabletop up to the Volcanoes. In short, *hijo,* I fear you will have to travel to. . . . Lavaland."

"L A V A L A N D? M A L P A I S! The Badlands?! *Madre de Dios!* Are you certain, Don Cuervo? Lavaland has long haunted Coyote dreams, for I have heard my father and my mother tell of the travails and trials of the trails to Lavaland: the ever-hungry Black Snake Road; the foot-cutting miles of Malpais and lava flows; the carved and pictured lava rocks of Boca Negra and Rinconada Canyon; the shaking, vibrating, twisting, buzzing bravado of Rattlesnake.

"There in the lava beds where Horned Toad and Lizard dwell I have seen the Sun red against Black Mesa and I have heard the distant peents and preents, beeps and spee'iks of Nighthawk's searchings. I have dreamed of Goatsucker's haunting cries at dusk. I have heard Thunder's clamor in his speaking with Lightning. I have watched Raincloud's darkened dance as Cloudburst, and heard the rush of brown-walled water down Arroyo. And I have heard stories of the snow which blinds there. I have watched Moon, high in the clear, starred sky of spring, linger over the loneliness of Lavaland and watched her weep. And I have heard Wind carry forth that weeping. *Híjola!* Holy Mother of God!"

"Yes, Lavaland is a distant and dangerous place. But it is a place of beginnings, of sources, of causes and of answers.

"You have heard of the once dancing and still holy rocks where all animal conformations, shapes and sounds, were first patterned? Where spirits and shadows formed into prototype and archetype? Where our Human cousins traveled for visions and embodied them in petroglyphs? Where, in those long ago days, people and animals worked and played together without strife, cooperating in comfort, respecting the differences and the similarities of life in all its forms?

"I can help guide you there—out West Mesa way. To Lavaland. Back to storied beginnings and to your destiny. The memories of your future. Yes, Raven will guide you to Black Mesa, to the Volcanoes and the sacred rocks. Guide you back to the imaged myths that picture who you are, and how and when you howl. But you will have to talk to others. You will have to listen to many voices. And not just the words. But the texture and timbre of your other cousins' tellings. Ask them about their voices. Try to speak like them, assume their voices. And in listening and empathizing perhaps find and define your own unique ability to howl again.

"This is a crucial time, Coyote, as you well know. So

can I be assured that *you* are sincere? You are not merely pretending, Coyote, my most curious constant and changing cousin. *Vámonos! Córrele!* Let us go then. Go then. Go. I sing of your journey:

Caw, Caw, *córrele.*
Caw, caw, come.
Come Coyote, come.
Huehue. Huehue. Huehue.
Howl Huehue. Howl Hue . . . hue.
Howl Coyote. Howl. Howl.
Coyote howl. Howl Coyote.
When Coyote howls,
When Coyote howls,
When Coyote howls,
Hear our own soul's singing.
Create in Coyote's creating
Our own creating.
Sing in morning.
Sing in night.
Sing in life.
Sing in death.
Sing in yearning.
Sing in mourning.
Sing in hunger.
Sing in mournful celebration.
Sing in Volcano's spewing roar.
Sing in Coyote craving.
Sing of Coyote change.
Sing of Coyote constancy.
When Coyote howls,
When Coyote howls,
When Coyote howls,
Then, Coyote, then,

We howl with you.
When Coyote howls,
When Coyote howls,
We howl tooooooooo.
Coyote. Come. Come
Come Coyote. Caw.
Caw. Caw. Caw.

And so Raven stretched and preened and shook his morning-misted wings. After rearranging his feathers he lurched forward and flew from his river roost through the Bosque branches of cottonwood and olive tree. He flew, cawing and calling, down the brown curling water along River's bank and pointed the way to the beginning of Coyote's journey Westward to Lavaland. Raven knew. Raven knew.

Raven flew high over the Bosque toward Oxbow and Big Arroyo, taking in all the Valley's morning stirrings. He called Crane, Goose, Muskrat, Duck, Kingfisher, Heron.

"Gaw, Gaw, Gaw! Caw, Caw, Caw! Coyote! Coyote is Coming. *Allí te watcho!* Coyote is Coming. Coyote is Coming," cried Raven. "He has lost his howl. He looks for his howl. He searches for his howl."

And River echoed Raven's call. And Bosque echoed Raven's call. And Arroyo absorbed the waves of sound: "Coyote comes, comes, comes. . . . Coyote comes. *Mucho ojo Amigos. Mucho Ojo! Escúchame! Todo el mundo cuidado!*" And everyone listened. Everyone heard. And everyone knew of Raven's cawing. Knew of Coyote's coming.

CHAPTER TWO

Long before morning I knew that what I was seeking to discover was a thing I'd always known. That all courage was a form of constancy. That it was always himself that the coward abandoned first. After this all other betrayals came easily.

—Cormac McCarthy, *All the Pretty Horses*

Coyote, following Raven's flight, trotted along the river's brushy bank. His bristled, glistening coat was brilliant against the morning colors of the bosque and his breath puffed forward in small, disappearing clouds of crisp morning air. Coyote could hear the river sounds of morning blending into an orchestration of approaching autumn. Nearby he heard Duck chattering and clucking in the shallow brown marshes of the ditch as its waters merged and melded with the muddy embankments of the river and the adjacent big marsh of the Oxbow.

There salt cedar and duck grass and marsh plants were plentiful. And there marsh gasses blurped and burped and bubbled in the mud. Horsetail rushes and cattail clumps protruded from River's expansive sheeted surface. Muskrat dove down into his muddy hole. And Carp, gulping at Waterspider, surfaced, his large back fin causing the waters to ripple out into patterns seen last night in Cloud's ringing of Moon. Beaver was long awake and hard at work. And Coyote jumped at the splat of Beaver's tail hitting the marsh water.

Coyote was thirsty and hungry and his throat was dry. His stomach began to cramp, and little muscle spasms said "Eat, eat." And he softly yelped and whimpered an internal prayer for help. An inner lamentation of longing. It was no time to surrender to this new fear at his pitiful raspy attempts to howl.

Coyote's eyes followed Duck as she rose off the river water and the morning-mirrored expanse of the Oxbow. Duck splattered about and then lifted off the water, upwards toward Raven.

Muskrat plopped his wet, river-bed head up from the brown rippling backwaters of the river flowing into the marsh.

"Is that you, Coyote, come to my muddy banks? Are you here for your morning ablutions? Do not think I am stupid enough to provide your morning meal. Raven's alarms have disturbed the morning stillness. But I wish to walk along the mucky banks of my home here. So how can I be of assistance and see you long gone from this swimming hole I call home?"

"*Almizclera, hola. El ratón, como le va en la agua fría!* Your greeting is welcome, albeit a bit hard to understand amidst all the burbling and bubbling of the water around your moistened mouth and showery, water-glistening, spiky-haired head. You appear to be in the midst of your own morning bath. But then you bathe all day long, do you not? Swim. Dive. Swim. Surface. Disappear. Surface. Now you see you. Now you don't. Your ears must be as waterlogged as your soggy voice. And what about the ice which cometh? What about that long day's dive? I need some quick advice. Can you stay above water long enough for that? I remain curious in my crisis and know nothing of your muddy hole home. I know only that I have lost my howl. Have you heard that through your plugged-up ears?"

"But of course. *Seguro,* Coyote Boy. Ah, ah, you simply need a good long gargle, Coyote. Your voice is merely overused and needs some lubrication. Watch my Muskrat remedy. . . ."

Coyote, quizzical and curious, stood on the marshy bank and watched while Muskrat opened his mouth for a swallow of water and then tossed back his water-slicked head for a long, wet gargle through which his words and voice garbled forth:

Muskrat must gargle, Coyote.
Muskrat must wet his whistle, Coyote.

Muskrat must soothe his throat.
Wet and water outside.
Water and wet inside.
Ah, so smooth and nice.
So smooth and nice. Ahhh.
Wetness is all. Wetness is all.
Gargle. Gargle. Gargle.
Good gargle. Good gracious.
Good gracious gargle.
Water soothes all, Coyote.
Water soothes all.
Water soothes a tortured throat.
Water calms the savage beast, eh?
Have a good gargle, Coyote.
Have a good gargling day!

"Muskrat Al, my little mousse-headed swimmer, you perk up my spirits with your ratty, rambunctious, rambling good-gracious day ways. Might as well laugh as cry, hard as it is. But you do bring a smile to my face and some clarity to my crying eyes. *Bueno, bueno hermano,* I'll try it."

And so Coyote splayed his front legs apart and tucked his head down for a good mouthful of water. He managed to get enough to hold in the back of his throat. Then he did it. He gargled. Or tried to. Rather than getting his voice back, Coyote choked. He gagged in his gargle and coughed a cough almost in Muskrat's face.

"Ho, Coyote, you clown around so much. Now you are giving me a good rat's laugh. Do you think you fool me with such antics of feigned innocence? You don't quite have the technique down yet, do you? No, not sagacious Coyote Man. Even so, hypocrite or not, just gargle each morning and I'm sure it will restore your howl to its best volume. Even two gargles a week will do. A singer like you must take care of the pipes, you know. *Hasta luego!"*

And before Coyote could quite stop coughing, or pretending to cough, Muskrat was gone, back beneath the water, leaving only the wet bubble and swish of his disappearance. Muskrat had some good advice, Coyote had to admit. My oh my, Muskrat would make a wet and watery meal! He would prefer something toastier. But Muskrat was right, Coyote did come from a family where singing was all important. A gargle a day might not be a bad regimen.

Coyote's mind turned to remembering his family and their times together. He remembered how he used to sound, how he could yap and yip and bark and howl out there on the mesas along the arroyo's edge. Out there among chamisa and mesquite, the saltbush and cactus, the yucca and Russian thistle. Out there with the Coyote community, his parents and his sisters and brothers. They would wait until the stars had moved along their vast heavenly way and the Big Dipper was turning low in the sky and then they would howl at the stars and at Moon. They would howl in Coyote chorus, "Huehueeee. Hoooowl. Hooowl. Hooowl." He would howl alone in a head-swirling, starry-songed solo, "Hooowwwlll!"

Jackrabbit would run from them, but not fast enough. Not smart enough. And they would chase Jackrabbit close to the den, and bark and howl the lessons of the hunt, and Moon was right, things were right, and it was good to be Coyote. His first howls weren't as strong as his parents', but his voice was young and strong and full and it carried well on the wings of Wind through the early morning darkness. When he and his family howled, their songs blended in desert and river, sand and water, in a choral serenade. All the Coyotes were proud. Coyote could tell. First one, then another would stop their own barking and yipping and yapping, barking and chanting and singing, and just listen to each other. Voices on the colors of night. Voices on the crisp aromas of early morning. Coyote could see the mutual pleasure and pride in the wide-mouthed smiles and in the way the others would tilt their heads and listen as Wind carried their cries out and back. Out to Moon and Sky. And carried it back changed by bouncing it off the yellow-shadowed face of Moon. And Moon would smile, reflected even in the glistening whiteness of their fangs. And Wind "approoooved" and said as much in his own singing.

Coyote remembered such things. But last night and this morning, all that had disappeared, and he was alone. Alone. And feeling strange and unable to make much of any sound at all. Nothing except his silenced and whispered sighs. His ardent yips. His subdued whines and yelps. Where it had all gone Coyote just didn't know. What happened to his full-throated song Coyote couldn't say. All of that fair springtime with family, with Jackrabbit and Moon and Wind and Stars had now disappeared. Gone. Gone. And the going was silent and mysterious. The demarcations of a day. Then. Now.

Moon knew. Wind knew. Coyote knew. And Raven . . . he at least knew how to help, how to offer advice, how to point the way. Could he sing it Coyote would offer Raven a song of thanksgiving for his assistance, his advice, his counsel.

Reassuring Raven.
Rapacious Raven.
Ravenous Raven.
Don Cuervo! Pájaro Grande!
Pájaro de colores de la noche!
Gracias. Gracias.
Thank you, Raven. *Muchas gracias!*
I watch you caw and cruise . . .
Caw and cruise your sturdy way.
Cruise and caw through the morning sky.
I am thankful for your help. I am thankful.
Ravenous Raven.
We hunger and hunt together.
Rapacious Raven.
We travel together searching all.
Reassuring Raven.
I follow your call.
I come. I come.
With your black blessing I come.

Then Coyote looked beyond and around Raven and did a doubletake when Duck turned into two Mallards, circling overhead, circling, their wings whistling through the sky just over Coyote's head, intercepting the extending line of Raven's steady, slow-winged way.

Two or three long quacks reached Coyote in greeting. He raised his head and set his ears just right to catch and listen as Hen and Drake circled and then set their wings for landing in the Oxbow's splashy marsh. They were beautiful in their splendid companion colors—Drake vibrant and Hen subdued. Beautiful in the speed and grace of their flight. Coyote momentarily forgot some of his troubles as he watched them extend their legs and push their wings hard against the air for landing.

Yes, it was Drake and Hen and they were chattering and quacking rapidly to each other when Coyote temporarily lost sight of them behind the Cattails that speared skyward out of the Marsh. Coyote honed in on the chattering, what he knew as greeting calls become feeding calls, and he picked up his speed in order to greet them himself, talk to his waterbird cousins, and ask them for advice. They would be wary, he realized. There had been recent mistakes. He was Coyote, after all. He was the Coyote they knew. Coyote of the wanting, seductive smile.

But he could convince them of his need and his sincerity this special River morning. He could. He regretted his earlier indiscretion when he had tried so crudely to mate with Hen and her sisters. They had not taken kindly to his engorged, impassioned penis feeling to him like a hard feather floating out on the water, trying to tickle Hen's own yearning. Drake would not forget that, especially. Coyote's escapades. Coyote's capers. But there was an excuse. Coyote was Coyote—and Coyote was young and impulsive, acting on the motives of his first spring. The urges of Coyote essences. Compelled by, well, by Coyote callings.

This morning's meeting would not be without embarrassments. But Raven's advice must be heeded. Coyote must consult everyone, including Duck. So Coyote turned and trotted toward the chattering, feeling his feet slush into the marshy water. Horsetail Rush stood erect in ringed and segmented stands—each wand-like frond telescoping beyond itself, extending upward, ever upward. Horsetail was as old as the Volcanoes. As old as anything in the landscape. As old as River and Marsh and Oxbow. Horsetail Rush was at the beginning. Stories said that First People, even Coyote, first came to this place through the passageway of Horsetail Rush. The others came through the Rush tunnel too. Through the hollow center. Came in segments, each group in each compartment. Coyote admired Horsetail Rush and its capabilities. Its endurance. Its survival. And Horsetail Rush leaned and bent with the water and the wind in salute to Coyote as he passed along.

Cattail waved above Coyote's head, brown and round and erect, and, like Rush and Reed, reminding Coyote Boy of his past passions with Hen and with others. Reminding Coyote of his yearning for Coyote Girl—wherever she might be. Reminding him of passion and lust. Longing and love—and adventure, always adventure. Perhaps Hen would not remember Coyote's amorous intrusion and not scold him too much. Perhaps she had not even told Drake. Possible? Impossible.

Soon the sound of the Mallards was very near and Coyote stuck his head beyond Cattail and Rush and through Willow at the edge of River's backwaters and there in a still pool, right there was Hen . . . and Drake. Coyote watched for a time. Hen, swimming and clucking, looked as beautiful and alluring as ever . . . almost. Drake decidedly dampened some of Coyote's amorous intent. Drake would make a fine meal, but Coyote could not think of such things right now. His old instincts had to be redirected for the mission at hand. He needed to talk to Drake and to Hen, to both of them. Ask them a few questions. See what they could say about things. See if they had seen or heard Coyote's howl. Learn if, in their winged journeys, they had noticed any shifts, any changes along the River. Coyote doubted if they ever flew over Lavaland. But perhaps they knew of waters to the west. Even past the Volcanoes. . . .

The Mallards saw Coyote's head peeking through the willows, his tail blending in with the cattails and reeds and his long snout reaching out much too close for comfort. They changed their feeding chatter into more rapid quacks of warning and alarm and swam further toward the middle of Marsh. Coyote, although young, was, they knew, a good swimmer, and quite impassioned in his past pursuits of Hen. But their distance on the marsh calmed them—as had Raven's earlier introductions. Coyote was coming along. And Coyote was now here.

Coyote got as close as he could and stepped further into River—just for a drink, because his morning thirst was strong from trying to howl most of the night and part of the early morning. As he lapped the soothing waters of River he watched the ducks as they paddled against the current, holding their spot against the flowing waters, stationary and strong amidst the rippling current. Coyote stepped back, repressing his old urges of pursuit. His old but abiding appetite for life. His hunger for death and lust and love. His abiding longing. His relish of that very longing. Coyote's hunger to howl in hunger.

Then Coyote looked up all of a sudden and pulled his head out of the water, his long tongue still dripping with the refreshing river water. River splashed against Coyote's thirst and hunger, against his yearning maleness. And, relying on his characteristic wiles, Coyote spoke—acting as though he had just then, by accident, happened to notice Hen and Drake. It was his habit to act so. A habit hard to kick.

"Well, my friends, good morning you two river romancers—Drake and Hen, my waterbird cousins. How's the swimming out there? Come closer and let us greet the day together. How are you, sweet Hen, *querida?* Where are your sisters? Have you heard about my serious misfortune? Did you hear Raven's morning call? Have you heard about *pobrecito* Coyote's trouble?"

"Coyote," quacked Drake, "do not speak so ingenuously, so charmingly now, here in front of Hen. I know of your past flirtations and motives. But, yes, Raven came before you. Even so you did not startle us. We saw you some time ago, clopping and slopping through Oxbow and Big Marsh, slushing around Cattail, Rush, and Reed, poking your head through the willows and brush there. River told us too of your coming. The swimming is just fine out here. For ducks. So you have lost your howl? And, yes, even we noticed its absence in the night. It was bothersome not to know just where you were roaming and what mischief was leading you on."

"It is good to know that you too listen for my howl, though what you hear is not especially what I intend, nor do I howl for Hen in quite the way you infer. But it is good that we are agreed Coyote should howl. Raven is directing me to ask all my cousins for help. Maybe if you tell me about your quacking and chattering and chucka, chucka, chuckering, I can learn something about my own howl—the how in the Hell, the how and the hell of howl. The nature of it. Coyote is Coyote. Constant Coyote, you know. But Coyote is changing. Changing Coyote too."

"Coyote," said Hen, "it is strange that you ask me about such things. My past discussions with you have been prompted by fear and attempts to resist your wantonness. My sisters feel the same way. You remember the last incident of your wayward manners. Notwithstanding your youth, until you apologize I have no advice for you, no sharing of insights about our talking and quacking and chucka, chucka, chuckering, as you describe it."

"You are right, of course, cousin," said Coyote. "And I apologize. To you. To your sisters. And to Drake. To Duck and to all ducks everywhere. I have not really thought about what it means to be Coyote or to be Duck, I confess, until now. So, yes, I'm sorry for my past youthful indiscretions. But sounds are plentiful along River this morning and perhaps my howl is with you. Have you seen it? Do you know why, suddenly, I can't howl this strange day?"

But Mallards chuckled softly to themselves, talking quietly about the probability that this was just another of Coyote's tricks. So they chattered and laughed to themselves. Soon they decided, however, that Raven was pretty reliable. Raven wouldn't fool them over this. And he could still be seen in the distant dawning sky, slow and heavy against the pushes and shoves of wind and wing. Looking for some little edge forward. Already seemingly tired, heading toward Arroyo.

So Hen and Drake decided, talking it over briefly, that even if this was a typical Coyote ruse they would play along with Coyote. For they understood the terrors of not being able to be Duck, not being able to utilize all the essentials of their nature. And they shuddered at the thought that suddenly one late summer Coyote couldn't howl. Coyote might never howl again for them to hear him, and in him hear echoes of themselves.

So Drake said, and Hen nodded her head in assent,

"We accept your apologies, Coyote, and we are willing to try and help you. Let us hear you try to howl and maybe we can give you informed advice. Just lean back in your usual way and yell as if events were happening naturally. And we will listen."

So Coyote sat down and tried to howl. He tried so hard he lifted one paw high out of the marshy water. He tried so hard he put a crick in his poor neck. All that came forth was a kind of sucking gurgle. A residual gargle. Much like Muskrat's burbling. Much like River's lapping of waters against the sedge along Marsh's edge. Much like Marsh Gas's burps. Hen and Drake smiled widely, saying, "Coyote, you can't even whine right, let alone howl. Your voice sounds rather embarrassing, more like you are breaking wind than crooning. Mr. Cool Coyote, we have a lesson for you. Pick Horsetail Rush there to your right. Pinch one end and place it in your mouth and blow softly, placing some of your longing and desire into that breath, that expiation."

"Well," replied Coyote, just catching his breath after his exertions, "that will take some assistance. Couldn't you two pretty *patos* swim over here closer and help? You can trust me. I'm in dire straits here you know."

Drake and Hen chanced it and swam over to Coyote. Drake picked Rush and Hen pinched one end with her beak and offered it to Coyote. Coyote thought during this assistance that once he did get his howl back, this would be a good trick, a lure to use again. But now he had to keep his word for he was indeed worried. Drake and Hen began to sing:

> Horsetail Rush sing for Coyote.
> Rush whistle and whine.
> Rush whinny whinny whinny.

Rush show Coyote the way back to song.
Whistle and whine and whinny.
Whistle and whinny and whine.
Whistle and whine.
Whinny, whinny, whinny.
Horsetail Rush sing for Coyote.
Horsetail rush sing Coyote back to ancient days.
Rush sing Coyote back to his beginnings.

"Blow now, with feeling, Coyote," said Drake and Hen in unison, and they held Reed up to Coyote's lips. And he blew. Rush whistled and whined and whinnied for him. And Coyote listened to the melody; he listened, and he felt what he heard. And he thought he heard all of the rushes and reeds in the Oxbow and along River's edge vibrate and sing along with him. He thought he heard echoes of Volcano's first pushing of hot lava through Earth's crust. He thought he heard echoes of First Male and First Female.

We sing with you Coyote.
We whine for you Coyote.
We whinny with you.
We sing and whine and whinny for you Coyote.
Remember Rush.
Remember Reed.
Remember Rush and Reed.
When you whine.
When you sing.
When Coyote howls.
When Coyote howls.
Whistle with the Male organ.
Whistle with the Female organ.
Sing of the Yucca medicine's magic.
Howl of the changing voices of young boys.

Howl of the changing voices of young girls.
Whistle and whine and whinny and sing and howl,
Coyote, Coyote, Coyote.

Then Drake and Hen took Rush from Coyote's mouth and congratulated him. "See, Coyote, Rush will help you when you howl. And we will help you too." And both Mallards strained their necks and quacked and squawked at the top of their voices in a long staccato string of noise become song to Coyote's ears.

He almost had to shut his ears with his muddy paws. But he realized the rudeness of such a response. So Coyote listened and the sound mixed and echoed with that of Rush and Reed, River and Marsh lapping and rippling around him. And he liked what he heard and felt what he heard and knew he would remember what he heard.

Duck quacks for Coyote.
Duck quacks for Coyote.
Take Duck's song Coyote.
Take Duck's song Coyote.
When Coyote howls.
When Coyote howls.
Duck quacks Coyote.
Coyote, Duck quacks for,
When Coyote howls.
Duck quacks and chucka chuckas.
Duck chucka, chucka, chuckas and quacks.
For Coyote. For Coyote.
When he howls. When Coyote howls.

Coyote liked the quacking, chucka, chuckering clamor. He liked the quacking, cacophonous clamor. Coyote liked the Whine of Rush and the Quack of Duck. And when Drake and Hen had finished Coyote tried to offer up his best expression of appreciation in what sounded, a bit surprisingly to him, something like ". . . ck you," ". . . ck you," yes, that was it, "Quack you. Quack you." And then they all laughed and chuckled and enjoyed the effects of the morning lesson, the morning's music.

"See, Coyote, you will remember us when you do find your howl. You will remember us and this good time together as friends."

And when Coyote laughed what came out was a long quack, shrill to be sure. Decidedly a quack. But Drake and Hen did not take such ventriloquisms as a mockery or an insult. They took it for what it was—their influence on young Coyote.

Then Drake began to worry. Then Hen began to worry. They realized that Coyote could now use this knowledge to fool them in the future. They would have to be careful. They would have even more to worry about. Because a Coyote who can't howl is not the same thing as a Coyote who could howl, but doesn't.

And Coyote saw the worry on their faces. Coyote realized he had gained a new power, one he could use against the very benevolence of Duck.

"Sincerity has its own rewards," thought Coyote to himself.

"Look here, *Chapito.* Listen up, Coyote," spoke Hen. "We admit you're pretty good now at imitating us. But you shouldn't be so bold or naive to do it for other motives in the future. We know Duck when we hear Duck. We know those Human duck callers. And we know Coyote when we hear Coyote. And we can tell if Coyote imitates Duck. You are welcome to use the sounds of Duck when you howl. But know this: you will never be a decoy of any effectiveness."

"You can be sure of that, Coyote," declared Drake.

"It is different for me," said Rush. "I can sing only with another's breath. But I see the point of the argument here and I whine and whistle much the same for celebrations as for betrayals. Anthems and dirges, you know. I can play them all."

Coyote reassured Hen and Drake, Rush and Reed and the listening Cattails and others that he would accept this gift and use this gift only in the spirit in which it was given.

But you never know about Coyote. You know? You just never know. Rush really didn't know when Coyote's breath touched her. And Drake and Hen didn't either as they said their goodbyes and swam back out into open water and lifted their wings skyward, quacking their farewells back to their gregarious, solitary cousin Coyote. Flying into the distance, Mallards become Duck once again.

Coyote watched Duck rise into the sky, crossing paths with Sun's rays now tilting more directly through the trees of the bosque. Coyote turned from the reedy marsh and headed back along the big irrigation ditch to the mouth of the arroyo that fed River from Mesa rains and Spring floods. Soon Coyote reached dry ground and began to lope along. When he came to a barbed wire fence he shimmied under the lowest strand, which scratched his back, causing him to yap. A tuft of hair stuck to a wire barb. Coyote was more peeved than angry or hurt. "*Cowheateee!* I have no hair to spare." His voice surprised him for it still sounded reedy and somewhat like Duck's.

"This is a day to finish as soon as possible," said Coyote. But he knew this was only one small discomfort he would face this day. "Other obstacles must be met and other kinds of crossings await on this way to Lavaland," Coyote said to himself. And he looked up for Raven, who was now perched in a young cottonwood at the mouth of Big Arroyo. Raven was standing on first one foot and then the other. He opened his mouth frequently as if gasping for air, catching his breath. Raven was older than Coyote realized. He was no speedster. But, with all this talking and conferring, it was good Raven paused and waited for Coyote. Even as Coyote acknowledged his and Raven's mutual advantage, and much before Coyote reached him, Raven was in flight, headed up Arroyo. Headed West with the Sun glistening on his back. Coyote was used to crossing Arroyo, not heading up it toward West Mesa, and Lavaland.

Coyote both welcomed and dreaded the soft sand of Arroyo. It was hard walking. But it was cool. He was tempted to rest and maybe roll in such sand as this. It was a good spot and he marked his place on the trunk of the Cottonwood where Raven had perched. Coyote noticed all the tiny tracks in the sand and he could tell who had passed by: there was Roadrunner, his long tail dragging behind him now and then. There were Quail's fast little footprints. Beetle's and Spider's little lined pathways. And Lizard's circuitous ways. Small Sparrow's hopping. There were Human footprints with waffle weavings and strange designs. There were the odors and the markings of Skunk, and of Squirrel. And of friend Jackrabbit. And of sometimes enemy . . . Dog.

As Coyote looked up Big Arroyo he saw several elm trees dotting the center of the wide bed where water had rushed, willy-nilly, torrential and trickling, from the clouds and floods on the mesas. The banks were high and steep, towering much over Coyote's head. The sage and chamisa bushes on the top edge were hanging on for dear life, exposing their twisted, nude roots, reaching ever downward for precious water. "I know how you feel, *Señor Sage y Señora Chamisa. Yo, Coyote, comprendo."*

A part of the opposite bank fell and slid into the sandy bed, causing Coyote to realize how quickly sound and motion come from stillness. Rivers are born. Rivers die. Arroyos come and go in many ways. Nearby, Coyote saw a spreading desert gourd vine sending out its curling and wrapping tentacles over everything and anything in its path. It even seemed to have trapped and killed a number of tumbleweeds, now brittle and brown and scratchy looking. Coyote gave the gourd a wide berth. *"Buenas días, Señora Calabaza. Buenas días!"*

But most disturbing for Coyote was all the clutter and debris. Human debris. Odds and ends cast off by Humans. *"Ay Chihuahua! Chingada!"* Chunks of old wood. Pieces of brick and tile. Lariats of rusted barbed wire. Bottles and cans and plastic containers of all kinds and shapes and in various stages of burial and exposure, littered Arroyo. There were many random pieces of lava rock, too, black and porous, hardened in the transition from gas to solid, air bubbles and gas bubbles cast in stone. Captive. Stunted forever but waiting again for life, it seemed. It was a savage place. At once calm and ravaged with prophecies of other passages in the past, and forebodings of things to come. From up ahead. From the West Mesa. From Lavaland. It was a compelling and a foreboding route.

When Coyote rallied and turned to begin his Arroyo journey . . . there was Ground Beetle, standing on his head.

"Greetings, Ground Beetle. Have I met up with the Yogi of Beetle Gulch? Come now, is this any way to say hello to Coyote? Pointing your bug-brittle ass at the sky? Although hungry, I do not wish to swallow you, front or back. What takes you on your slow way this day?" Coyote queried. "I see by your wandering, lined little trail in Arroyo's sand that your fragile legs have not taken you very far. I hope your destination is not as far as mine. Are you not able to walk a bit faster? Will you not waste the day away standing this way?"

Beetle lowered himself back fully to the ground, pivoting and ratcheting his body around to face Coyote.

"Do not scoff at my morning habits, Coyotl, neither my acrobatics nor my walk. I heard Raven's morning commotion. He told me of your plight and asked me to advise you, regardless, Raven said, regardless of any of your old arrogant teasing. In the name of my own shiny-green blackness and of my cousin Raven's, I would only tell you that speed is not everything. I might add that distance is defined by many days, not one. And by many journeys.

"Remember that Beetles outnumber Coyote in kind. Beetles outnumber all others. Together this morning and millions of other mornings the Beetle bunch have covered the greatest of distances. As for my scratchings in the sand, my claws paint these designs for me and I greet Morning with my own patterns of beauty. An expert on tracking such as you should realize these things and respect them. I can run too. Not as fast as Millipede, my Lavaland cousin. Not as fast as lean-legged Coyote, I admit. But when needed I can run."

"Exacto! Sí! Sí!, but of course," conceded Coyote. "Forgive me, Beetle. I did not mean to insult you. And I appreciate what you say. I, too, am a ground goer, as you know, and the tracks which you make I do not always acknowledge. Please accept my respect for you and your family, for I know you crawl and fly and swim and creep and are everywhere. But tell me about your talking and your singing. For I am in much need of your opinion and counsel about my howl."

"Raven told me about your plight, as I mentioned. My songs are the songs of frictions and scrapings. Have you not heard me singing in the evenings when my love songs course along the wind? Here, listen. . . ," and Beetle moved his scraping hind legs against his lower body:

Beetle sings of Coyote's coming.
Beetle sings of Coyote's running.
Beetle sings of Coyote's howling.
Run Coyote.
Sing Coyote.
Howl Coyote.
Run, Sing, Howl Coyote.
Beetle walks with Coyote.
Beetle sings with Coyote.
Beetle gives his song to Coyote.
Beetle is here.
Beetle is there.
When Coyote howls,
When Coyote howls,
Beetle hears.
Beetle sings.
Beetle howls too.

Coyote listened to Beetle's ancient voice and it scored itself hard into Coyote's head and heart. Beetle stopped his stridulations and, after a few beats, redirected his attention to Coyote.

"Remember, Coyote, Beetle's singing comes from across vast stretches of time and family history. Beetle sings even before birth and this is part of my blessing to send you on your way. Songs must come from the spirit as well as the physical anatomy. Won't you try my song in this way when you howl?"

Just then Coyote had to scratch behind his ear so he sat down and raised his rear leg to his head and took a few passes at his ear with his foot.

"*Órale, cabrón, órale* . . . . Do you continue to insult, Coyote, just because I sing with my legs is no reason for you to engage in such embarrassing mockery. Your old ways are incorrigible. Be gone with you."

"No, no, *Oye, Amigo Escarabajo,* Beetle . . . please," said Coyote in an unusually grainy, rasping way. I merely had to scratch this ear itch. And if my voice is scratchy like yours, believe me, Beetle, believe me it is not in mockery. I take all of your fine advice to heart and carry it with me up Big Arroyo and when crossing Black Snake Road on the way to Lavaland."

"Good. I accept your explanation. Now go, Coyote. I must get back to my morning exercises."

"*Ho, Don Escarabajo!* A sense of good health and humor still resides in you. *Que bueno,* Ground Beetle. *Bueno.* My hunger rises and I must go. Raven is tired from lack of sleep. He will nod off if I am not diligent."

Coyote was hungry for his howl. But hungry also for breakfast. So he waded on through the heavy sand toward the stand of three elm trees and their distant shade. Coyote thought he remembered Raven flying there. Coyote had only gone two or three hundred yards and reached the spot where Arroyo flared out to touch the adjacent mesa of mesquite and chamisa, when Coyote heard Quail and her titillating, accented morning calling. He paused and looked around, listening hard. He felt something tickling his paw and looked down to find he was standing in the sandy, moundy home of the Black Ants. Black Ants were out in full force, out in the hundreds. Busy lines of Black Ants passing in and out of the hard hole which was the doorway to their underground tunnels.

"*Ay, ay ay! Ay Carumba! Las Hormigas!* A thousand apologies, amigas and amigos. I'm just passing through—off to see Quail. You do hear Quail calling me, Ant?" And Coyote shook Ant off his leg, watching him fall back into the swarm of workers. Only the faintest little yell and the most imperceptible cushiony clunk could be heard. And Coyote spoke quickly to Arroyo.

"If Raven looks for me, tell him that I leave you and your many crawling creatures for a short time, Arroyo," Coyote reported. "I hear a breakfast call from Quail, a growing favorite of mine."

"Be careful, Coyote," Arroyo answered. "Because Raven has charted this route for you. Do not stray too far into the warming sands of my sister Mesa, for only my more moist pathway will sustain you on your westering this difficult day. I will have to tell Raven of this right away, *rapidamente, ahora!*"

But Coyote was already trotting out of Arroyo into the morning Mesa. Sun was well up in the sky and the sand was warm on Coyote's feet. Quail, on a clump of sagebrush, was singing *una canción alta y clara,* and

Coyote soon came near to her. He crouched down to listen and to watch. Her plump white-aproned gray body was stately atop the bush. Her black topnotch arced forward over her russet-brown head in sympathetic vibration to the melodies of her song—at first a soft coo and then an accented crescendo.

Then she changed to a short cluck, followed by a screech like a rusty hinge scraping on an old shed door. On her wings she bore a white-striped chevron with the utmost confidence. And the white feathery streak behind her dark eyes stressed her watchful duty as sentinel for the covey.

A line of pygmy Quail children followed a pear-shaped mother beneath the sagebrush singer who had caught Coyote's attention. Coyote was tempted to pursue the parading family. But he was captivated by the song which came from atop the sagebrush clump now tinted almost turquoise in the Sun's mid-morning rays.

Now Quail sang in single, whole notes beginning in a crescendo, sustained, and then diminishing. The song was echoed in the distance by other quail, less worried in their watching because of the air-borne messages amplified from atop the sagebrush. Coyote was captivated by the song and couldn't help admiring it in a new way this particular day, forgetting somewhat about the soft growling of his stomach.

Raven had seen Coyote's detour out of Arroyo and flew to the top of a nearby telephone pole to watch and wait for his presently more willful than wily cousin. Even this, Raven rationalized, would teach Coyote something for his journey—a trip which, Raven lamented, Coyote still resisted making with full commitment. But Raven knew the ways of young-old

Coyote, timeless Coyote. They had journeyed together before, sidekicks in another moment, another beat of earth's motion and moving.

Quail saw Raven in the distance and knew Coyote was crouching close by. He was dangerously close to the nearby houses. For while the Humans who lived there protected and even fed Quail, they feared that Coyote wanted to eat their pets, their small house cats of various common and exotic breeds. Quail knew such things and she was bold in such assurances. As Coyote crawled closer to Quail's perch, the rest of Quail's family scurried toward the houses. One or two of the covey broke cover and flurried into the air, unnerving Coyote only for a second as he watched them set their wings and coast, gliding back into the chamisa and sage that bordered the yards and property around the houses.

Quail was the first to speak.

"Coyote. Coyote. What brings you to this part of the Mesa this morning? Coyote, have you changed your home range—or should we, if you plan to stay in this vicinity?"

"Quail. Quail. *Querida.* My fine singing, clear-voiced friend. I am enjoying your song this morning. Have you not heard that I go in search of my howl, for it has either been stolen or disappeared? Has not Raven informed you of this? I seek some counsel because I suffer from a strangeness this morning which I don't understand. A few yaps and yelps, a yip and a whimper or two, a gargle here and a cough there, and this kind of soft-voiced conversation. That's about the extent of my voice this day.

"With Raven as guide I am en route to Lavaland. I was lured here by your fine music and the melodies in it. Muskrat offered his throat medicine. Duck and Rush and Beetle send their voices with me. I find that your song has its special strengths and enchantments in it. *Qué linda pajarito. Qué bonita tu canción."*

"Cállate Coyote. Your officious, devious ways have no limit. I know flattery and its motives. Do you really expect me to believe this as you hunker and crouch and crawl along with the hunger of your stomach and the desire of your chops so obvious in your yellow eyes? I know too about your moves on Duck and all the others, you wayward Casanova. Quail is not so stupid as to fall for this concocted yarn of yours. Lost your howl, indeed!"

And Quail chirped and chuckled and laughed, confident in her high perch which Coyote could never reach.

"True enough. My hunger is strong and it is not just a stomach hunger. This is a full-fledged, five-alarm *salsa caliente y picante* crisis this day. If you do not wish to offer up yourself or any of your family to give me the physical nourishment to continue, then at least give me some pointers which might come in handy. You know I admire you, *mi querida*—in my way."

"Well, I'll tell you to follow a route far away from those houses over there. You know that much. You can kid with Quail much easier than with Humans and their dogs. And many dogs live there believe me: labradors, shepherds, rottweilers, schnauzers, spaniels, poodles, collies, terriers, malamutes, afghans, mongrels, and on it goes. And knowing that you are a male, Coyote, those dogs would just as soon eat you for breakfast as you would gobble down a nest of our children or a couple of our plump parents.

"Moreover, Coyote, given past times with you and

your family, any benevolence of mine, especially as guardian of my covey, must be limited. It is to our benefit to know your condition. And I have heard certain strains of your story in Raven's voice from afar. But Raven has not talked about you directly with me this morning. He watches us yonder from that telephone pole, do you not notice? No doubt he listens to the Human messages in the humming wires. Perhaps he hears other things too.

"See him turn his head down, just so. We count on hearing you howl each night, early and late, for that way we know your location and your mood. And now that you mention it, I have not heard Coyote's howls in the recent past. As we feed, this late summer becoming fall, we have noticed that your family has pretty much departed and left you alone. Can you not howl for that?"

"But of course. I miss the others and I look for them on my journey. But I am to discover my own way at this time. That you must know as well."

"Try to talk to Hawk. He flies great distances, from the River west to the Foothills and to the Volcanoes. From the River east to the Mountains. He sees everything. Must you cross Black Snake Road yet today? Hawk sometimes follows and counts the carnage there. So seek him out if you can. Hawk stares at us even now. Take a jaunt over there and see him on your own terms. Even his shadow scares the hades out of me!"

Quail kept on chirping and talking to Coyote—so much so that Coyote couldn't get a word in edgewise, neither of assent or question. Quail was clearly stalling, ad libbing, just allowing the rest of her family to settle as near the houses as possible. Quail wouldn't even pause for a breath of air. And the talk was becoming not only more garrulous but more gratuitous. Coyote knew he had to be on his way even amidst such smooth-throated talk. He heard again and could feel in his throat Beetle's raspy scratchings now blending with Quail's silky song. Another fine gargle would be nice about now.

Quail was right about the houses, though, and he turned back toward Arroyo. Quail had accomplished her objective and she yodeled to Coyote as he went along.

> Coyote, te, te, te.
> Good luck, luck, luck.
> Coyote, te, te, te.
> Good luck, luck, luck.
> Coyote, te, te.
> Good hunting, ing, ing, ing.
> Coyote, te, te, te.
> Good traveling to, to, to.
> Lavaland, lavaland, la, la, la.
> Lavaland, lavaland, la, la, la.
> Coyote, te, te, te.
> Te, te, te, la, la, la, la.

Raven watched as Coyote approached Arroyo. Raven cawed with some slight warning in his voice as he rose from his pole-top perch and flew further West: "Follow Arroyo. Follow Arroyo, Coyote. *Vámonos! Vámonos! A la Veca!"*

Coyote would do just that. He re-entered Arroyo with mixed feelings of trepidation and thanksgiving. In cutting back after his visit with Quail, Coyote now had passed far beyond Arroyo's mouth and was well into the dry river's main channel. Some few salt cedar and cypress trees and clumps of willow still spotted the sandy bed and clustered along the edges of the channel of the main waterway. The stand of elm trees was now only a few yards from Coyote. He sniffed low and he sniffed high for any sign of Mouse or Cottontail Rabbit or maybe Jackrabbit. Jackrabbit would be a much preferred morsel of nourishment, morning, noon, or night. And what Coyote smelled was appetizing beyond his daydreaming. Mouse and Jackrabbit were nearby. So was Lizard.

It was Bluetailed Lizard, *Lagarto,* who first darted across Coyote's path. Lizard, in his blur of blue and gray, was so fast that Coyote heard more of his speed than actually saw it, for Lizard was running through some gourd vines and the leaves and brush held in the spiraling runners of the plant. "Such fast running, Lizard. *A dónde va?* I commend you in your exceptional speed and agility. If you look for Beetle, I pity him unless he has time to throw out his defensive powers. Lizard, I have caught you in the past only to find your tail twitching beneath my paw and beneath my disappointed, glowering, eyes. Such cleverness I also admire. Would that I could run faster than my own tail. Leave it behind and then generate another one. Perhaps you could leave Gourd for a time and we could play, or just talk. *Qué dice, hombre Lagarto?"*

Lizard stopped to stare at Coyote. The stripes down Lizard's back were straight and long and black, standing out against the gray back and cream-colored belly. It was a color combination which, in its way, approximated Coyote's desert camouflage. Large circular earlike holes, set far back on Lizard's head, allowed him to hear well, Coyote believed. Perhaps they were gills.

Coyote was curious. *Lagarto's* long fingers, tipped with tiny suction cups, allowed him to climb anything and go in any direction. Lizard opened his mouth and started to complain to Coyote when he was subdued by a large, moving shadow and an air-borne, high-powered growl and hiss.

Coyote first thought it was some terrible sound Lizard was making with his tongue. Then the shadow passed over them, revealing a giant, colorfully striped, tear-shaped bird. For a second Coyote thought it was the mother of all Quail, come to scare him into ultimate and final submission. But it wasn't a giant Quail. It was something else.

In the wicker basket suspended beneath it was a Human. He was pointing toward a large, wheeled, road machine parked beside a gravel road in the far distance. Two humans! "*A la máquina! Qué pasa?* What is that, Lizard? What, pray tell me, was that orb?

"One of hundreds of such air machines, Coyote. They sail over Mesa and Big Arroyo and the Oxbow every morning almost. They come from far up River and they usually land right over there near the Palisades. They groan and hiss and fart and generally disturb the peace. Even their colors are outrageously loud for me. They seek not to blend in with the sky, but to stand out. However, the blue ones, I do admit, have a certain attraction for me. I have yet to see one match the vibrancy of my own tail color, of course.

"I just watch them sail by here from the shade of a chamisa bush or from my gourd vine. It's my best cover, long and stringy—and my lookout. These hot and flaming balls have their festivals, you know. Their own versions of *Fiesta*. They dance in the sky like the dancing rocks of old. Like the boulders of Lavaland, once catapulted hot and high and now fallen quiet and cool."

"*A la mode!* It's hard to comprehend such things. There is more than we know to be found in heaven and earth, they say. And *Don Lagarto,* Lizard runner, you are wise much beyond my imagining, what with your sense of colors and knowledge of the Human sail ships. That one scared the piss out of me, and I mean it. *Mira, hombre!*"

"Such is your way of complimenting a friend, Coyote? I am in no mood for such smooth talking, insincere stuff and nonsense. *Cállete la boca. Cállete.* Piss and be gone. Be on your way. The sooner you leave, the sooner you can bid hello to all my sun-bathing, rock-climbing Lizard friends in Lavaland. And there are some big ones there, let me tell you. So tell them good day with some respect."

So Coyote, still intrigued by the shadowed ball of color that carried the Humans, continued on his way. What a fartful flier!

Lizard would have been a nice breakfast tidbit. But the morning menu had other things in store. And soon Mouse came running along. When he saw Coyote he stopped quickly and tried to turn. But Coyote was upon him. Coyote had Mouse, squeaking, squeaking, fast in his paws. There was no time for discussion, for Mouse was already swallowed before he could say a word. Coyote thanked him for the offering up of his little life.

Mouse would make a fine first course. And then would come Jackrabbit. So Coyote decided to rest close to the hole where Mouse was headed. There he would wait for Jackrabbit. Coyote knew much about Jackrabbit's habits. And Jackrabbit was nearby. Jackrabbit was, in fact, just a few yards away, crouching down, his long ears pulled down alongside his body. Coyote could smell him before he actually saw him. Could smell and see Jackrabbit's fresh, dark, hard, round pellet scat. Mostly, it was Jackrabbit's scent that gave away his hiding place.

Jackrabbit knew Coyote was near. Knew it hard and with hurt when Coyote grabbed him. Jackrabbit let out a frightening scream that resounded across the mesa, giving pause to Quail especially. Jackrabbit twisted and jerked and struggled so that Coyote couldn't concentrate, couldn't hold him. This scream of Jackrabbit's, any other day, would just have come to Coyote's ears as a victory, and Jackrabbit would have been dead, chewed, and swallowed! Coyote knew Jackrabbit's chucking ways, his deep-throated growl in the spring when chasing Jackrabbit Girl for mating. And Coyote knew this high-pitched shriek, this death-cry of Jackrabbit's which now pierced his ears and made Coyote think mournfully of his own lost howl and made him . . . , made him . . . let Jackrabbit loose. Jackrabbit lay on his side, looking up at Coyote. Coyote could see the panic in Jackrabbit's eyes. Could feel the parched throat as Jackrabbit swallowed hard, daring not to blink, hardly believing that Coyote had decided not to eat him.

This day Coyote admired Jackrabbit's screaming as if his life depended on it, which, of course, it did. Jackrabbit, in the split-second of his first screaming, when he felt Coyote's clutches, had already reconciled himself to being eaten. His scream was as much a goodbye as a cry for mercy. So when Coyote let him go Jackrabbit couldn't believe it and he hopped as high as he could hop, up and away, away, away from Coyote.

Jackrabbit ran to a safe distance, his rear end high and his back legs pumping hard. Soon Jackrabbit stopped and shook himself all over, especially his long ears and his black tail, and then, situated on the slope of a small sandy incline, he turned to thank Coyote and discuss this strange change in Coyote's nature. Coyote watched Jackrabbit's long, translucent ears tilt slowly down. Sun was shining through them and Coyote could see the blood circulating through those donkey ears that now shone pinkish.

"Caa, Co, Coyote," stuttered Jackrabbit, "you gave me a scare. Are you losing your hold on more than just me? What's wrong? I should be thankful, but I hate to see you not being yourself. I need to depend on certainties such as Coyote death."

"Jackrabbit, you are right. This is an unusual turn of events and a strange day for me—and now for you too. The short of it is this: I can't howl. And, as you see, I can't really hunt. My hunger is greater than usual—for food and nourishment such as you and Mouse provide, but also I hunger for my howl. I couldn't howl in the night. I couldn't howl this morning. I can't howl just now. Your screaming reminded me of my troubles.

"You are at least still Jackrabbit, still *El Conejo Grande, El Koko,* the great Kokopelli's heir, doing what you do. Running. Screaming. Resting. Always luring me to chase after you.

"As for me, I'm not myself, not able to do what a Coyote must do, not able to be what a Coyote is. Lucky for you, I suppose, although I see your point about depending on certainties. Howling was to me a certainty. Now I am thrown into doubt and, in releasing you from certain death, I've let you go into greater worry. But this is a temporary condition I'm sure. Raven, as you no doubt have heard, leads me to Lavaland where the Earth itself knows ancient wisdom about its own howls—and mine. As an adversary who knows me best, what's your opinion about this condition of mine?"

Jackrabbit then hopped upright on its hind legs and looked around. "Coyote," said Jackrabbit, "since we have called a truce of sorts, let us walk into the shade of that elm tree *allá, en el centro del arroyo,* and sit in its shade for a while. Raven will allow you this conversation, I'm sure. For the distance to Lavaland requires some resting along the way. He will soon circle back here because he knows you and he knows me and how we depend on each other. But this time-out may puzzle him."

Raven did see Coyote and Jackrabbit talking and he knew that this was a unique moment, one which Coyote had staged, and Raven knew why. He expected to see Coyote chewing on Jackrabbit by this time. But Raven too had heard Jackrabbit's scream and its echoes of Coyote's past and potential howl. Raven knew too that the shadow and snorting of the hot air balloon and its Human fliers had frightened Coyote. So Raven began circling back to find a resting place nearby.

Sun was high in the sky now and Raven would have to prod Coyote to keep hurrying along. "Caw, caw, caw. Coyote, Coyote, Coyote," sang out Raven as he circled, pestered all the while by two small obstreperous diving blackbirds. Raven headed for one of the many large electrical power poles, whose numbers were starting to increase in number. Tall, orange-brown, creosote-stained scaffold poles, reinforced for the heavy wires and high voltage current. Hawk was over there already, surveying the landscape and the escapades of the day. Looking for Death.

It was indeed a strange sight there on the edge of Arroyo: Jackrabbit, looking much older than his five actual years, and young Coyote walking together into the shade of Elm tree. Jackrabbit's large hopping rear haunches and shorter front legs made him appear to limp across the sand—more in line for permanent rest and retirement as *un conejo viejo* than for racing as *El Senor Jack, El Gran Koko.*

His long, black-edged ears still shone, and these long, twitching shafts of skin and muscle made him look even lopsided.

Coyote noticed too how unusually long Jackrabbit's tail was and how it matched his ears with its black-tipped marking. There was a story here, Coyote knew. Coyote wondered how such speedy prey now hobbled so slowly. Perhaps he had developed blisters or broken a rib. Coyote would like to know the story of just how Jackrabbit came to be this way. No doubt Kokopelli had something to do with it. Him and his flute. Him and his high-frequency, alluring mesa, valley, and mountain music.

Coyote still looked around, always aware but his head had a new droop to it and a certain snap and spirit was missing from his movements. Sun shone warm on Coyote's back and the shade of the elm was cool and comforting to his weariness and his worry.

"Coyo, if I may call you so, just as you call me, although wrongly, Koko, I wish you would just call me Jack, after all these intimate years of chase and death. I do know you better than you imagine and although you might think I would like to change you, especially in your appetite constantly to chase me down, my advice to you and to all of us here on Little Mesa and in Big Arroyo, in Bosque and yonder in the Foothills of the Volcanoes and the Lavalands of Black Mesa, is to hold hard to our identities, our personalities, our natures, our essential selves. Constancy and Courage go hand in hand. Something of a *dicho, qué no?* Not too preachy for your tastes, I truly hope.

"What you sense this strange day is change. It is not just seasonal change from warm to cold, from summer to fall. It is more, too, than the change from youth to adulthood and maturity and the aloneness which that will mean for you as the others leave and you make a new life, finding yourself, finding others, finding a mate. It is not just the urging for a companion and for parenthood of your own. These are all forces at work on you this strange late summer day. But what you face—what we all face—is what I'll call the weakening of wildness. The threats to our wild natures, to who we are, the essences behind our pictured and storied selves—these threats are many, prevalent, and insidious."

"*Qué Koko! Qué Conejo! Qué Jack!*," interrupted Coyote. "You wax philosophical and a tad religious this day. This is somewhat surprising, coming from you, although we have never really stopped to exchange ideas in discourse. Your knowledge has a familiar but puzzling ring to it. I sense that what you say is so and I would like to try and repeat it in my howl, imitate you—if I could howl—when I—when Coyo *sans* howl—howl. (I even have trouble speaking today, as you can see.)

"I have much to howl about, as you can guess. In your screaming and yelling back there I heard much of the music of what I miss, the fervent will to live, to live wild. Tell me more of your thoughts about this allegiance to wildness, this present-day anemic wildness."

"I listen to much, as do you, Coyo. But never too much. Our ears are critical to us both. These things of which I speak are in the air. Others are talking about them too. Has not Raven, your guide, spoken of this as he leads you onward to Lavaland and your search? Let me explain what I am hearing and seeing more and more in my circles of hops and runs and jumps these many years.

"Few of my family die of old age, as I'm sure your family can testify. And yet I've run a good race here on Little Mesa. A few generations ago all of this good and glorious desert—from the Bosque to the Volcanoes—was wide and spacious, free and wild. Those who came before us were able to walk and run, to talk and howl, to rest and sleep within the old order of the days and nights, the skies and the seasons.

"The changes of Earth and Nature were constant and your urgings—this time in the changes between the summer of your youth and the autumn of your growing youthful maturity, which will repeat itself many more times than allowed me—are constant and repeated in all of us. In the animals and in the birds, the trees and the plants, the insects who walk the sands and the waters, the fish and others below the water. In River Heron. In Dragonfly. In Muskrat. In Black Ant.

"Once this very Arroyo ran from the Foothills to the River, filling the marshes of the Oxbow. There was no Black Snake Road dividing the Mesa from the Foothills. There were no ditches or rocked and wired, engineered embankments for 'water diversion' and flood control. Flash floods were natural and we knew their ways, many of us being swept away in the roaring rush and foam of immediate destruction—and replenishment.

"There were no Human dwellings, no houses and businesses, no shopping malls like the sprawling rooftops that line the Black Snake Road where the careening Motion Machines crush and kill my family, your family, and the families of all our cousins each and every day, each and every night. There were no Sky Balloons to frighten us with swooshing gasses, flame burners, and ominous, shadowy eclipses."

"*Koko, por favor!* Please Jack," whimpered Coyote, "I must cross the Black Snake Road. Spare me any frightening details. Raven tries to build my courage, not deflate it. He knows of the loathsome carnage but does not dramatize it for me. And I need encouragement from you as well. Accentuate the positive kind of thing, you know. Optimism. Faith in the future. *Viva la Vida!* You drift toward pessimism here. And for one whose life was just spared!"

"I speak only of things you should know, Coyo, regardless. They will give motive and form to your howl in its constancy and in its modulations. There were none of these things built by and for Humans, those wrapped up, hat-wearing walkers and drivers and fliers whom we see and marvel at, and try to avoid. No speeding motion machines on the Black Snake Road to run over us, to kill and to maim us. No flying balls of bright color to frighten us with their up and away launchings, their gliding shadows and gaseous growls of hot air. No white, cloud-streaking machines in the air.

"The older, earlier Humans knew us in harmony, hunted us, yes, but respected us, carved our likeness on the rocks of Lavaland. These Humans we see now on Little Mesa shoot at us for fun! Many of my kin have been killed by one Child Human who comes out here each day with his .22 rifle. No doubt you have heard his plinking. Perhaps you have escaped from him. He rides a silly little dirt bike and wears a profane hornet-shaped hat. He is the bane of my existence here. Let me die in your jaws any day rather than from his sophomoric bullets. For he would kill me and forget me. The hunters, the real hunters, are no more. You and I respect real hunters, right?

"This place was ours in the long ago, and we were who we were. 'That which we are we are,' I like to say. These Humans and their ideas for turning and taming us into pets or obliterating us began settling in this place and began building on it in the days of your grandparents' parents. It is a short time in the natural rotation and cycle of Sun and the seasons. It is for us our lifetime and the lifetime of those before and after us. We can't stop these Humans and their buildings and mechanical intrusions. So we must adapt. Jackrabbit adapts. Roadrunner adapts. Quail adapts. We become dependent. Our diets change.

"Even Coyote enjoys a wayward house cat, does he not? Our test, our challenge is to hold on to the wildness which has always defined us as independent in our ways but respectful of natural forces—the elements, the seasons.

"These Humans are dangerous in their actions, their evil, their goodness, or their indifference. They place carrots for Jackrabbit and for cousin Cottontail outside their condominiums, their swimming pools. They arrange apples for us in their lawns. They throw seeds out for Quail along the edges of the Human fun fields, the tennis courts, their basketball courts and softball diamonds.

"And Dog, your relative and sometimes a dangerous enemy to us, walks with them or runs loose to chase us. Jackrabbit must beware of Dog even more than Coyote. And you know how you yourself avoid Dog.

"These Humans set traps, as you know, to protect their cattle along River. Forgive my anger and frustration but these are dangerous times, times of creeping cities, times of civilized changes which promise to kill us if we are not careful."

"Yes, Koko-Jack, I know some of this and share your feelings of fear and frustration. Not the whole story, for I am young. But I have heard my family talk of such things, of the need to move further away from these Humans and their good/bad intentions. I have seen the Humans' way of death. And my late litter brother pulled himself from a trap, leaving his leg. But what does this have to do with my howl and where it has gone? With Moon and Wind and my journey to Black Mesa and the sacred, pictured rocks of Malpais?

"Your howl, Coyo, your urge to howl, and your ability to howl—my motive and energy to scream and cry when caught and the tone and timbre and color of it—is very much related to this process, to these changes and this strangeness which is your cup.

"When Coyote cannot howl a crisis is at hand. At least you still want to howl, want to maintain this voice of yours. Tell me, Coyote, have you ever considered why you howl? Consider: how did it happen that you howl in the first place?"

"Well, Koko, I have howled much in recent past times, even in my young life . . . but I never considered it until today. This the day my howl is hiding. I howl to howl. It is what makes me Coyote. It is my laughter and joy. It is my tears and my sorrow. I have heard stories from the others, the old ones, about how our howling came to be. Those stories go way back and you hear them in the very howling itself—my howls, Coyote's howls. Most say I howl because I brought Death into the world. You have heard that story, I know. That's a serious matter. Death. And I don't deny my hunger for more space, more food, did lead to some proposals for Death to come and take the old people into Sky for a long visit. When they never returned, I was exiled and destined to howl forever. Even so, that story is a bit too simplistic for me. I howl for many reasons."

"No doubt, Coyo. But to find your howl again, you must know, I think, where it comes from. Imitation of the voices and songs and screams of the rest of us will help you empathize. But you must, as they say, find your own howl, your own song, your own voice. It is, you know, still somewhere inside you. It was a gift to you as you yourself recognize. In the very oldest of times it was decided that sounds needed to be heard and different sounds were placed within us for our use—to help us tell how we feel—to show pleasure and displeasure to talk and sing and pray and to warn our friends and to learn from each other.

"Those first forces who decided this made us all speak the way we do. You will learn soon, if you don't already know, that women speak in special ways, as do men. But then you are an expert in such matters, I know.

"My parents didn't believe that story which says that in those first days we all spoke in similar ways.

Jackrabbits, they insisted, were always Jackrabbits, so even though we all show fear or pleasure, or yearning or hunger, or loneliness or ecstasy, our voices, our sounds have always been different. You too have heard such stories of beginnings and the ways in which arrivals are the same and different. I believe in both. Although our sounds are not the same, we both have our howls and our need to howl—as you well understand.

"Raven advises that you travel to Lavaland and to the Sacred Rocks of Black Mesa. Raven has his reasons and knows much. I have seen the great Kokopelli's image there and know his rabbit spirit. I know that in those early times, still in evidence in Lavaland, we spoke more clearly to Humans and aided them in their pictured languages, too.

"My identity with Kokopelli, the great humpbacked flute player, is strong, for I have seen him. Heard him. You will see him, too, no doubt, in Lavaland. But you will not see him in quite the way I did. For he and I are one. In his music and song is news of good things—of food and of fertility. He combines the best of the ancient Humans with the best of Jackrabbit, representing the days when Humans lived here in greater harmony with us. He's full of vinegar, that Kokopelli. He values the life force for sure. As you do. Optimistic? He's optimistic. His passion for procreation, his hunger for life, is every bit as great as yours, Coyote.

"To a certain extent Kokopelli now gives me my knowledge. Writes my script. Gives me my myth. Plays my song. Wards off my despair. But then, who was here first? Jackrabbit? Kokopelli? Our myth? The pictured rocks of Lavaland will help you sort out these things. They will enlighten you. It's a necessary trip, *compadre.*

"River has its knowledge. Arroyo has its knowledge. Mesa has its knowledge. Lavaland has its knowledge. Jackrabbit has his knowledge. I know with Raven this important thing: that to find your howl you must look inside yourself. Find your rock, find Coyote Rock, and it will point the way to this, as will your journey there. Still, you must discuss these things with others closer to you than I am. Trust me. You know trickery when you see it. I am sincere."

"Jackrabbit, you are both wise . . . and nervous, I see. You wish to be going along, I sense. I am grateful and, as you sense, I am still hungry. Interesting that you know that from my actions without me saying so."

"And from your eyes, Coyote. You hunger for both your howl and what determines it, and for the strength and stamina to howl. So with your permission, I'll just amble up the Arroyo and leave you to your further journey. We owe our gratitude to Elm Tree for the comforting shade provided us during this time together. Go with my song, Coyote. Go with the strains of Kokopelli's raucous and alluring music, his flute strains. He knows the music of Rush and Reed. Go with the soft and sweet sounds of Rush and Reed, of Horsetail, oldest of old vegetation. Listen, Coyote, listen to my song in your Lavaland journey:

> Jackrabbit gives his song to Coyote.
> Jackrabbit gives his scream to Coyote.
> Go to meet life Coyote.
> Go to meet death's coming Coyote.
> Sing of going and coming.
> Sing of that which changes.
> Sing of that which stays.
> Sing the song of life Coyote.

Sing the scream of death Coyote.
Go with the music of Kokopelli.
Go with Jackrabbit's going along.
Go with Jackrabbit's hopping.
Go with Jackrabbit stopping.
Go with Jackrabbit running.
Jackrabbit sends you his song.
Jackrabbit sends you his song.
Jackrabbit sends you hope and life.
Coyote. Coyote. Go Coyote. Go.

Coyote could feel that mid-morning Sun was approaching him and he confirmed this by looking skyward. He squinted at the bright blaze of Sun and then looked at the outline of the spot of shade shift into a smaller circle around him. The hunger in his stomach was stronger and it spoke to him with a growling sound. He listened. He felt the sound within him. For a minute he thought it was a howl. Maybe his howl rested in the shade inside him. So he tried to turn his growling stomach into a howl. Only a yelp escaped amidst the growling of his stomach.

Coyote thought about what Jackrabbit had said, and what his other brothers had told him during his morning journey. The voices and advice of Raven. Muskrat, Duck, and Quail, and Horsetail Rush.

Coyote looked down Big Arroyo and could see some distance away how it flared out to meet the river—how the cottonwoods and willows and Russian olives and cypress trees began to thicken to form the dense Bosque. He looked further to see the wide marshes of the Oxbow. Then he looked up Arroyo and saw how its banks began to grow higher and in the far distance of the horizon framed the Volcanoes of Lavaland.

He counted five Volcanoes—three set off to the left, and larger. And two smaller ones to the right. Would he have to journey to all of them? Which one held his destiny? Sun's path was his path now—toward the Volcanoes, the Malpais of Lavaland. And Coyote remembered past memory his hearing and knowing of that dark and ancient place. The Malpais blackness was deep and dull, as black as Raven but not as shiny.

Raven and Hawk had watched Coyote talk with Jackrabbit from their high resting place. All during Coyote's talk with Jackrabbit, Raven had talked with Hawk. Some things they agreed on, other things they argued about. Hawk was full of himself and his own opinions. Hawk was a hotdog flier, a hero of his own occasions. Raven had his special moves too, however, though they were more sedate. In the distance of his Bosque home, Raven looked longingly at Cottonwood. Cottonwood's leaves would turn soon. Autumn was coming golden. And it would be followed by the deaths of Winter. Hawk talked much about death. Knew deeper secrets than even Raven about killing. "One must kill to enjoy one's prey, Raven," Hawk would rub it in, and taunt Raven now and again in their discussions.

The stark, bare branches of Cottonwood in Winter were like the ancient death-dullness of the extinct Volcanoes which had once glowed with molten magma spewing forth. Leaving the earth's core as moving, seemingly alive molten lava.

Soon Raven said goodbye to Hawk. Raven twitched his wing feathers and lurched skyward toward Coyote, who was still sitting in the shade of the elm, enjoying Arroyo's cool sand.

There was much to ponder and a great distance to

cover. Jackrabbit knew many things. And although he too had some tricky ways, Coyote could admire them and respect Jackrabbit's views. They had a long-standing history between them. Coyote knew Jackrabbit did not give up his life for Coyote's hunger without a struggle.

Raven's shadow first interrupted Coyote's thoughts and then he heard his brother's voice.

"Come, come, Coyote. There is no time to waste, for Sun is moving rapidly along its journey to Lavaland and beyond the Volcanoes. You must be on your way to the Foothills and into the Malpais and lava boulders by sunset.

"Follow Big Arroyo until it reaches the Black Snake Road. Once you make it across Black Snake Road and avoid the death of that place and the whining and whirring terrors of the speeding motion machines, you will be in the hills which rest and roll at the foot of the Volcanoes. Watch too for the giant power lines which hum their way to the top of the Volcanoes. Their surges of electric current will put you on edge, Coyote. I will not be far away. Listen for my call."

Coyote looked at Raven's dark body circling and calling above him. He raised himself, shaking himself from head to tail and regretting the loss of the cool dirt from his body. But Raven was right. Coyote looked up to see Raven's dark wings taking him far up Arroyo toward Lavaland. Pointing the way.

Coyote barked a reply as much to himself as to Raven and in the sound—which surprised Coyote in its faintness—could be heard Coyote's hunger and thirst and worry. A new feeling, a weakness and a longing to rest longer or perhaps sleep in the shade, crept along inside him, growling there in the shadows of his insides. But he shook himself again. He rose and marked the elm tree with his scent. Then he walked out into Arroyo, where the hot sand made him run. And as he ran he sang to Arroyo:

Arroyo. Arroyo. Arroyo.
I ask for your help.
I ask for your direction.
Take me to Lavaland.
Take me to Black Mesa.
Provide me with water.
Provide me with food.
Show me the way of Big Arroyo.
Show me the way. Show me.
Arroyo. Arroyo.
Up Big Arroyo I come.
I am coming your way, Arroyo.
Arroyo. Coyote is coming to Lavaland.
Coming over the sand of Arroyo's water way.

Coyote traveled along Arroyo for some time. The Sun loomed round and red in his eyes, forcing him to look downward and away. Blue-Tailed Lizards skittered through the mesquite off to the side and disappeared into the rustling leaves and cast-off vegetation. Lizards were everywhere. Then, out of the corner of his eye, Coyote saw Mouse's twin, Ratonito! He too scurried about. This time out from behind a piece of old dry cactus stem. And Coyote caught Mouse, who knew, like his twin, that it was his day with Death, his appointed time, and he said so with an acquiescing squeak. Coyote knew that death sound well, a kind of mysterious sound of reluctance but of cooperation and assistance in the ways of the desert. So calm in comparison with Jackrabbit's scream. Coyote was so hungry that he thanked Mouse only after he had swallowed him.

> Thank you again good Mouse.
> Thank you for this Mouse morsel.
> Thank you for your life.
> Your brave small voice goes with me.
> Your help takes me to Lavaland.
> Your way takes me to Black Snake Road.
> Your way takes me over.
> Your way takes me across.

Then Coyote ambled over to Cactus and bit off several of its fruits. The Cactus tunas Coyote loved. They served as a dessert after Mouse. "Mouse is not Quail or Jackrabbit but he is a cousin this day and nourishment for my travels," said Coyote to himself as he licked his lips, belched once, and resumed his running up Arroyo. "I thank my cousin Mouse, for his consent to help me. And I thank you, Arroyo, for helping me on my travels this day."

Soon Coyote heard a new and strange sound, one that he couldn't categorize in any familiar way. A sound eerie in its newness to his keen ears. It was coming from some distance up ahead, around the next turn of Arroyo's embankment, which was widening now as Arroyo began to flatten out into the desert and encroaching Foothills. He couldn't see the sound. But he could hear it. The sound seemed to hiss and hum and whistle and whine all at the same time. It had a siren quality of its own—while another siren sound traveled along it from one end toward the other, penetrating deeply into Coyote's sensitive ears. At first Coyote thought it was the power lines because the poles were starting to stand brown and high against the horizon. But it wasn't the power lines. It was something else.

Coyote noticed that houses and buildings were also increasing in numbers. One or two were close to Big Arroyo, with walls and portals extending up to Arroyo's bank. Arroyo was beginning to wash away at the foundations of these cement creations. And Coyote could see where rock levees had been constructed out of wire and lava rocks. "Those houses were either too close to Arroyo or it was coming too close to them during the last flash flood," thought Coyote.

Just then Coyote heard a faint but more familiar sound—a definite barking. It came from a large dog running in the distance. It was running toward him, a very large, dark dog. Shepherd? Doberman Pinscher? Labrador Retriever? Golden Retriever? Jackrabbit had warned Coyote, reminded him about dogs. Coyote recognized something of himself in them—in their barking and their running. But the barking against the hum and hiss and whir some greater distance in front of him was grating to his instincts, to his nerves. He started to run back down Big Arroyo but knew Raven and Jackrabbit and even Mouse would be disappointed in his lack of courage and resolve to finish his journey and reach his destination before sunset. So Coyote slowed down his run a bit and moved more to the far side of Arroyo.

The dog kept coming, and around its neck Coyote could hear metal tags clinking and ringing as it ran toward him. It was a cacophony of sounds, none of which Coyote enjoyed hearing. What these sounds meant Coyote had no idea. But they too disturbed his ears and set his sensibilities even further on edge.

In his attempt to keep the dog in view, Coyote had neglected to see another presence coming into Arroyo. It was a Human. And he was standing on a large, broken and cracked cement culvert, abandoned in Arroyo. The Human looked straight into Coyote's face and brought him to a stop. They stared at each other for a time—until the Human yelled out. His voice was shrill but loud, and Coyote heard his name repeated again and again: "Coyote. Coyote. Coyote." But the human was not yelling at Coyote. Not a greeting to Coyote. "Coyote. Coyote. Coyote. Right here looking at me." The Human wasn't trying to get Coyote's attention. There was alarm and excitement in the yelling and in the sounds, which Coyote recognized as Human language. Human words.

There was another Human running behind the dog—a woman, a girl who ran swift with her long dark hair flying and bouncing behind her. She was young. And she was beautiful. Coyote could tell. Her voice was beautiful too. A comfort, somehow, amidst all the commotion. She was dressed in a dark green short jacket. And she had a ski-band around her ears, and it pushed her hair back from her long forehead. She was slim and Coyote knew she, too, was a runner. He even thought of her as a slender roamer, a kindred spirit in some strange way.

The young girl/woman called out to Dog and it stopped running and went back to the woman who told it to "Stay!," and held it by its collar. Coyote looked again at the first Human, the man looming above him like a spectre, mounted atop the cement culvert and Coyote recognized some glimmer of fear and excitement and of longing and admiration in the Human's eyes. Then Coyote barked softly at the man. And the man spoke to Coyote:

"Coyote. Coyote. I see you. Coyote from across the Mesa I greet you. Coyote, Arroyo Runner, it is strange and so special to meet you here this day. Your wildness once was fully in me, and now you reawaken it. When, in the night, I hear you howl, it stirs my blood, revitalizes my soul in all its longing for knowledge and for courage in the face of the known and the unknown. Coyote, I greet you and salute you. But I fear for you here this close to Human dwellings, the houses, the highway at our back, so close. Its promise is one of danger. Beware, Coyote. Will you not turn back? If I wave my arms and clap my hands will you know it is to warn you, Coyote? I wave you back from this place, Coyote. Go Coyote. Go back and stay out there in your wild ways." And the Human man raised his arms and waved them at Coyote. Then he took off his hat and waved that. Coyote started to turn, and then he heard the distant, pleasing voice of the Human woman.

"Dad. Dad. I see him. I see Coyote. And oh how beautiful he is. Oh, how beautiful he is in his running. I will not let Rojo harm him. He knows Coyote. He knows. . . . His barking is strong and wild."

And Coyote looked past the man and looked hard and keen at the woman and thanked her and the man for such feelings.

Then sounds from above came to Coyote, penetrating his preoccupation with the woman, and he was compelled to look skyward to Raven and his cawing, interrupting cries.

"Coyote. Coyote. Do not waver. Continue your journey up Arroyo. Coyote. You must cross the Black

Snake Road to reach the volcanoes and Lavaland. The answer to your questioning, to your quest awaits you there. There is danger but I will guide you. But I must turn back at dusk. I must reach my river roost before sunset. Follow Arroyo. Do not turn back. Follow the Arroyo straight to the Black Snake Road." And Raven swooped down to urge Coyote with repeated cawing.

> Come. Come. Come. Coyote.
> Come Coyote. Come Coyote. Come Coyote.

Coyote looked once more at the humans, the man, and the woman, father and daughter. Then, with a silent howl he said, "Wish me luck. Wish me luck. I travel West to Lavaland."

The woman seemed to understand and she watched Coyote for the longest time, reaching down to pet her big red-furred dog, Rojo, now awakened to old stirrings of wildness, old feelings for Coyote. And the woman felt something very strong stir within her. She understood little. But she knew, too. She knew.

And Coyote dashed, undaunted, full speed toward the humming and whirring and hissing sounds emanating from the distance.

Coyote ran fast and soon came to the strange blur of moving objects whizzing and whining and slithering along. Road machines. Motion machines. There were many of them moving at speeds only Coyote could appreciate. Moving faster than Coyote could imagine. Faster than Jackrabbit. Faster than Duck. Faster than Coyote himself.

The motion machines were making howling sounds of their own. Maybe, Coyote thought, he remembered hearing such sounds in the far, far distance from his den by the Bosque. Or perhaps his father and mother had only told him about them. These sounds had come to him in memory or in dream and he recognized the dangers. Recognized Black Snake Road! Coyote could see Raven, who had already flown to the other side, high over the Black Snake Road, and had landed on another power pole. Coyote paused for he didn't know how to sort out the noises, the howls and the whines of the machines speeding by in front of him. He was a bit dizzy. He was thirsty. The energy provided by the morsels of Mouse was waning. And Coyote sniffed the air for the smell of water.

Water was near. Water was near. Coyote looked hard and saw a pool of water at the mouth of a gigantic steel culvert, similar to the one the Human had mounted. But this one was galvanized steel. It was huge. Larger than any Human-crafted object Coyote had ever seen. And it ran underneath Black Snake Road and attempted to channel Arroyo underneath Black Snake Road as it sought out River and Oxbow below. The dark culvert opened its gaping maw, as if ready to devour poor Coyote. He felt much worse than Jackrabbit might feel with Coyote breathing down his victimized neck.

The little standing pools of water were just off the roadway. More elm trees grew there. It was a curious oasis. Alluring and repelling. The noise grew louder and louder in Coyote's ears as he approached the water warily. He had to drink. His thirst was stronger than the discomfort in his ears. Such cacophony of sounds! Such awful noise! These whistles and moans of the Black Snake Road! But such alluring, necessary water.

Coyote reached the small pools of water. They were

muddy and ringed with moss. Coyote had just lowered his head and begun to drink when Roadrunner fluttered down from the branches of the elm tree. Sun was tilting low in the western sky, allowing a burst of red and orange light to frame the purple-black Volcanoes, now much, much larger in their closeness. Black Mesa and Lavaland were there. Waiting. Just beyond Black Snake Road.

Dove darted by over Coyote's head, hurtling fast toward River. Coming off an afternoon feed of seeds on Mesa. Dove knew the dangers of her own crossing. One large motion machine, one that towered much higher and was much longer than the others, barely missed splattering Dove into spiraling feathers. *Cuidado. La Paloma!*

"Others have died here, Coyote," sang out Dove. "Be careful, Coyote, if you cross. Black Snake Road counts many casualties each day and each night. Listen to Roadrunner. Listen to his advice."

Then Swallow, Tashchozhii, flew past in her looping swoops, looking for insects around the culvert and over the small pond. Swallow's angular wings and V-shaped tail swished through the air, and Swallow twittered her own warning to Coyote.

"I wish I could welcome you here, Coyote. And I do. But know, too, that this is a dangerous place even for a smart fellow like you. It is difficult even for me, for Swallow, to make the best of this place. But there are many bugs. Be watchful, Coyote. Be watchful. *Buena suerte!* Roadrunner knows what I am saying. Roadrunner knows."

Dove and Swallow could not talk at any length to Coyote. They were on the move and not a little bit surprised to see Coyote there this long afternoon.

Most of their greetings had been lost in the noise of Black Snake Road. Things seemed quite frantic to Coyote. And Black Snake Road hissed out a seductive welcome to Coyote:

> How are you Coyote?
> How are you Coyote?
> How is your howl Coyote?
> Howl with me Coyote.
> Howl with me Coyote.
> Hear my howl and hiss.
> Hear my howling hiss.
> Whine and swoosh and scream.
> Scream and whine and swoosh.
> Coyote choose your time.
> Coyote choose your time.
> Come cross Coyote.
> Come cross Coyote.
> Black Snake Road can make you howl.
> Black Snake Road can make you howl
> In Death, Coyote.
> In Death.
> How are you Coyote.
> How is your howl today?
> Whishhowllll. Hooooooowwwwlll.
> Whishhhhhhh . . .

Coyote couldn't be sure he heard what he thought he heard. He noticed that even his cousin, Roadrunner, seemed much more nervous than remembered. They had met before in Arroyo and on Mesa. Their encounters were the stuff of legend. The stuff of cartoons, even, although Coyote knew nothing of that. Coyote had seen Roadrunner do battle with snakes before.

Even Rattlesnake. Coyote and Roadrunner knew each other as hunter and as prey.

Roadrunner always did seem to flit and jerk his way along. He would extend his neck and his head and then, with his long tail stabilizing him, churn his legs into a spinning wheel of motion. He would fly a short distance. Then he would hit the ground running. His tasseled head gave him an unkempt look. His blinking eyes seemed all the more pronounced beneath the coral and blue eyebrow of skin which slanted back and away from them.

Roadrunner had always struck Coyote as somewhat comical—whether as antagonist or accomplice. But now Coyote was especially glad to talk to him, even if he was in more of a snit than usual. There was a different kind of frenzy in the atmosphere here. Little peace to hear your thoughts or the words of others. Roadrunner was running first to one side of the pools and then to the other, head bobbing and tail twitching in a combined see-saw, palsied fashion. Roadrunner was the first to offer a greeting.

"Coyote. Here you are. Here you are. You're late. Late. You know what they say about you and it's true. True. You are always coming along, coming along. But you are not always arriving. So you've come to Black Snake Road. Raven spread the news of your coming. So I'm not surprised. I am not surprised. I regret it but I'm not surprised. We do what we must. We do what we must. This is a busy, frantic place. Busy place. Busy. These pools of water are at a premium. But water is not scarce there by your Bosque home. You travel far—and not just for water, water."

"True, Roadrunner. I left much water at River and at Oxbow. But I am also very thirsty from my day's travels. And I have further to go—to Black Mesa, to Lavaland, to the Volcanoes. I hope to speak with Lava-rock and learn the whereabouts of my howl, whether it was taken by Moon or by Wind or just what has happened to it and why. The Lavarocks know of first things. Know of my motive and my destiny. Are you at home here by Black Snake Road? All of this whizzing, buzzing commotion seems to agitate even you. But is this why they call you Roadrunner? I had always thought you made your own roadways."

"*Qué Vato!* Ever the kidder, Coyote. Coyotl the kidder. The roads I run down and across and along go much beyond this winding blacktop. I know the dusty roads, the trails and paths of our cousins. Our cousins. And it is there that we have met, as you well know. As you well know. But I am here now and know certain things which will help you here at Black Snake Road. So be grateful Raven has enlisted me for this roadway rendezvous, rendezvous.

"What's in a name?," Roadrunner continued. "You are called many things, Coyote. All of our cousins go by many names. Many names. We name ourselves and we don't. Do actions make for words? Words make for action? You know the adages. *Dichos* for the day. For the day. Roadrunner is as much a nickname for me as metaphor and myth for my own life script as your ancestors well know and you know too in your own blood's churnings. Have you not said as much in past howls? Past howls? But I have adapted my ways to fit in here temporarily. I visit the houses behind you and recognize their rooflines as well as my desert roads. Desert roads."

"Where is Rattlesnake, your nemesis, Roadrunner? Certainly he does not frequent this place. Bluetail

Lizard still scurries back in Arroyo and sends his own raspy hello with me. Has your appetite for snake abated here? What form does Death take here, pray tell?"

"Death is everywhere along Black Snake Road. Everywhere. Even Rattlesnake does not fare well here in his crossing. Now, as autumn approaches, Rattlesnake seeks out the crevices of the Black Mesa, the ledges of Lavaland. He awaits you there once you cross the Black Snake Road. Rest assured. Rest assured. That is, he awaits you *if* you reach Lavaland. Silent snakes rest here as does Bluetail Lizard—and Horned Lizard. Horned Lizard will see you in the Foothills. But here Death travels in the form of the Black Snake Road. Its appetite is never ceasing, which you will learn if you do not heed my advice in the crossing which awaits you. Which awaits you."

"Horned Lizard? You mean Horned Toad, my small, ugly, white-bellied, complacent friend? I look forward to talking with him and maybe flustering him into his magical bloody-eyes trick."

"Raven has asked me to advise you in such things, Coyote. Black Snake Road is the place of much killing, much slaughter and mutilation. Death travels the Black Snake Road day and night. Raven knows this well, for he finds many of our cousins scattered up and down here each and every time he journeys here. These objects of noise and motion, the Humans call them vehicles, automobiles, trucks, and such names. In their mechanized noise they kill whatever crosses too closely in front of them. At times they swerve, not to avoid us but to hit us. It is not a pretty story, Coyote. Not pretty.

"These Motion Machines crash wantonly into each

other, killing the Humans themselves, their own drivers and operators. Many of your relatives who have come this way, like mine, have been victims. This is why I consented to advise you when Raven called me and told me of your efforts to reach Malpais and Black Mesa. This is why."

"Raven tells everyone that I search for my howl and that I am coming this way? I welcome your help in this crossing. I have much speed and keen eyesight and know I can maneuver between these whizzing creations. Just point me in the right direction and say the word when I should dash across. I am willing to gamble with *La Muerte* for we are acquaintances. *Vamos! Viva la vida! Viva la muerte! Estoy listo!*"

"Well, Coyote," squawked Roadrunner, "you and Raven are curious fellows—all for life and all for death. One definition of courage, I suppose. I suppose. But your life is more important than your howl at this point. I wish to hear you howl in life—not death. It might not seem so crucial to you at present. But first things first. Sometimes your bravado seems fake, if I may so observe. But that's what makes you such an interesting *compadre.* In any event, I'm here to help you stay alive and stay out of Death's way on Black Snake Road. So I will guide you *under* the road, under the road, not across the asphalt surface and the eerie yellow lines running forever down its long back. In our time we return to Horsetail Rush Tunnel! Beginnings. Endings.

"You are to cross through the passageway provided by the corrugated steel culverts that course beneath the belly of the Black Snake Road. But that too takes its courage because of the loud volume of noise which reverberates and vibrates through each and every bone and muscle and fiber of your body and splits your head in two with a headache of sounds. A headache of sounds. Few are wise enough or brave enough to avoid trying to run across the top of the Black Snake Road and face this nerve-shattering, cavernous and cluttered lower crossing."

The hums of the Black Snake Road intruded again on Roadrunner's instructions, his plans for Coyote's crossing over. Coyote's aching ears doubted that any culvert noise could be worse than this. He would surely risk losing his hearing as well as his howl if such were the case. But the time had come. Roadrunner's next words were sober, and he spoke with unusual calm.

"If you have satisfied your thirst, Coyote, it is time now to travel through the culvert and its tunnel passage as it makes its way under Black Snake Road. Think of it as a rebirth out of death. Whatever gets you going. Allow me to send these words with you in your passage. They are the words of Roadrunner. Words of survival.

> We travel now together, Coyote.
> We travel now together, Coyote.
> Under the belly.
> Under the belly
> Of Black Snake Road.
> The spirits of all of our
> Road-traveling cousins attend us—
> Accompany us Jackrabbit, Squirrel, Skunk,
> Dove, Swallow, Hawk,
> Lizard, Possum, Raccoon, Small Snake,
> Rattlesnake, and the rest.
> May more learn of this path we take.

May all know that our survival
In the front of,
From the affront of,
Humans and their Motion Machines
Depends on the sharing of our wisdom.
We travel now together, Coyote.
We travel now together, Coyote.
Under the belly.
Under the belly of Black Snake Road.

And so Coyote followed Roadrunner through the culvert tunnel which ran under the belly of Black Snake Road. The initial darkness did not bother Coyote. He was used to traveling at night. Nor did the debris of old cans and bottles and tumbleweeds waylay him. He had seen such leavings back in Big Arroyo too. So Coyote dodged around pieces of desert plants and tree limbs and chunks of lumber, as Roadrunner zigzagged around objects and sloshed through small puddles of putrid, stagnant water. Coyote relished Roadrunner's trickery of outsmarting the Motion Machines. But Roadrunner was comical too in his own silly, sly-stepping artistry of movement.

Yes, Coyote admired Roadrunner and he appreciated his help. *"Gracias, Paisano! Gracias!"* Raven was doing some good work in preparing the way to Lavaland.

It seemed to Coyote that the Volcanoes were erupting. Such shaking surrounded him. Such clamor and clatter and roaring. The noise and vibration from Black Snake Road was making it hard to concentrate on his thoughts and he could barely hear himself think. He did hear Roadrunner squawk out a warning or two. There was Roadrunner jumping and dodging and dancing ahead of Coyote. Then Roadrunner turned his head and yelled over his extended wings which he was using in most ingenious ways to balance all of his high-stepping:

"Look at the orange hues of light in the distance, Coyote. Think of that. Think of that. Try to block out these evil noises. Worry not about what seems to be the shaking of all the earth. This is no earthquake. The Volcanoes remain quiet. It is just the Black Snake Road rumbling above us."

The few minutes of Coyote's culvert crossing lasted for what seemed to be an eternity. Coyote wanted to howl back at Black Snake Road. Coyote wanted to curse the unnatural abomination of it all. And he opened his mouth and howled a silent cry of anguish, for all he could hear was the highway howl above him. The noise above their heads was frightening, and the round walls of the culvert shook so much that Coyote's feet and legs tingled and ached even as he reached the glowing, red-lighted exit.

Soon, but not a bit too soon, Coyote followed Roadrunner out the other side and into Arroyo once again. The soft, moist sand felt refreshing. And even the clatter was diminished without the amplifications of the culvert. Arroyo fanned out wide into little washes lacing the Foothills, which were now intermittently glowing in the vibrant light of the sunset and dimming from the long shadows cast over the landscape by the towering Volcanoes and the Black Mesa. The flat, elevated Black Mesa extended out into the foothills like the fingers and paws of some giant primordial Black Bear or some prototypic shadow ancestor of Coyote. The fiery redness that spewed out of Big Volcano's cone was caused by Sun's setting. For a moment Coyote's soul was transported back to the most ancient days when such fire was real and not the illusion of light. Sun's explosions and its cosmic heat had once fired this desert and covered it with the spectacle of molten lava showering down from the sky, crawling forth in desperate search of the cooling waters of River, flowing forward on the Foothills to mark them with Volcano's footprints for all time.

Coyote had never seen such a sight in all of his young life. He was awed by the sublimity that faced him, surrounded him, and lured him onward into even closer connection and no doubt, confrontation with Lavaland. He knew this was an all-important journey, a once-in-a-lifetime visit to the place he would know and remember for the rest of his life. He had crossed Black Snake Road. Now Lavaland awaited him. Now his destiny was near.

It was Roadrunner who jarred Coyote out of the roamings of his reverie. And behind Roadrunner's squawking was Raven's cawing in the distance:

"Goodbye, Coyote. Goodbye, Culvert Runner," spoke Roadrunner. "Remember our adventures together this day. This day. Raven waits for you there on that high pole, and he is impatient. You are well aware that with the Sunset he must return to his River roost. He calls to you. But before you continue on the most significant and dangerous and profound part of your journey, remember Roadrunner's words. Roadrunner's words. To howl is also to listen and to know the voices of silence as well as the voices of sound. To know the music, the joy and the sadness of life, its good and its evil, you must also know noise. For harmony is defined by the contrasts of cacophony just as night defines day, life defines death, the ambitions and trials of youth define the successes and accomplishments of maturity. And you will succeed. You have come this far. You have crossed over. You will be able to meet your fate and to cross back an even wiser *hombre,* Coyote. It is, to be sure, all important to know how to howl. But it is equally important to know what to howl. To howl what is worth howling. So I say to you . . . , say to you . . .

> Roadrunner runs through the culvert with you,
>   Coyote.
> Roadrunner runs along the road with you, Coyote.
> Roadrunner runs along the Mesa with you, Coyote.
> Roadrunner runs along Arroyo with you, Coyote.
> Roadrunner outruns Sun with you, Coyote.
> Roadrunner runs in your heart and in your soul,
>   Coyote.
> Roadrunner runs with you in your running,
>   Coyote.
> Roadrunner runs with your howling, Coyote.
> Roadrunner runs with Coyote, Coyote, Coyote.
> Coyote run with Roadrunner.
> Coyote run. Coyote howl. Coyote howl.

"Thank you, Roadrunner. I begin the end of my journey now. I run across the Foothills. I run to Lavaland. Raven flies toward us. I must go. Remember your friend Coyote. I take your words and your wisdom and your serious, nervous, comic ways with me, Roadrunner. I owe you one, *compadre.* And I'll remember your own wiles next time we meet. This tunnel route outsmarts the clattering and whizzing Motion Machines. Just how fast do they go, Roadrunner? We are fast runners we know. But even our combined speeds are no match for them. This has been humbling for me. But it has been reassuring."

"They are so fast, Coyote, that they notice nothing and appreciate nothing. Nature blurs by them as they run through it or over it. But put this behind you for now. For now."

Then Raven flew closer into Roadrunner's and Coyote's ken—with his familiar cawing out of encouragement. There was a new urgency in his voice. "Come along, Coyote. Sun sets rapidly and the Lavarocks of Lavaland await you. Come along, Coyote. Coyote, come."

CHAPTER THREE

There they stood, ranged along the hillsides,
met
To view the last of me, a living frame
For one more picture! in a sheet of flame
I saw them and I knew them all.
Dauntless the slug-horn to my lips I set,
And blew.

—Robert Browning,
Childe Roland to the Dark Tower Came

I clamped my palms to my ears and stretched up my lips and shrieked again: a stab at truth, a snatch at apocalyptic glee. Then I ran on all fours, chest pounding, to the smoky mere.

—John Gardner, *Grendel*

Coyote looked up at Raven in his flight. Raven's calling steeled Coyote for the next push across the Foothills. When Coyote looked again at the Foothills, Roadrunner was gone. Coyote began to trot toward the Volcanoes, now large and looming and seemingly only a few minutes' distance in front of him. The Foothills were crossed by several washes and their sandy beds were cooling rapidly with twilight's coming. Sun was sinking lower and lower now, disappearing back into Big Volcano's central cone. Or so it appeared to Coyote who was captivated by the sight of the spectacle surrounding him.

Coyote knew that once he hit the lava flow of Black Mesa he would have to climb over the porous, rough and jagged Lavarocks and Malpais. Immense volcanic boulders were scattered randomly on the sides of the tabletop. Smaller stones, formed in Earth's core and thrust up from her innards, were dagger sharp. Then, once on the Tabletop of Black Mesa, Coyote would have easy passage for a time until he had to walk the final climb up Big Volcano's cone. Raven warned Coyote of these things, and Coyote had seen them in his dreams, for he knew of what Raven spoke.

Amidst such thoughts and the shifting feelings of reluctance and resolve, courage and fear, Coyote began to trot across the Foothills. He enjoyed the feel of the Foothills. Dove and Swallow still darted toward the river in their dusk crossing of Black Snake Road, now receding farther and farther behind him in its noises and blurring motion. Coyote paused to look back at where he had been. The length of Black Snake Road was startling to Coyote. For as he cast a long look in the line of the darting birds he realized how long and winding and encroaching Black Snake Road really was, wriggling there half-way between River, Bosque, and Lavaland.

Coyote shifted his feet, felt something round and soft, and heard a small voice of alarm. When he looked down, there was Horned Toad. And he was spewing and sputtering. He was so mad that blood was coming out of his eyes. For a minute Coyote thought he has squashed the poor fellow. But then he remembered Horned Toad's marvelous trick with his eyes. It was some ancient magic Horned Toad had learned in the course of his own life travels. And Horned Toad looked as though he had lived forever. He seemed straight out of the oldest of days. There with Horsetail Rush. There with Furry Mammoth. There with Saber Tooth Tiger. Around the Tar Pits . . . . Maybe even there with Tyrannosaurus Rex! The days when Volcano had been formed and had formed this particular landscape. Horned Toad not only looked old and crotchety, his admonition was that of the ultimate curmudgeon.

"Huehue. Huehue. Hey, hey, Coyote. I see red. I see red. My blood gathers knowing you more as a walking appetite than a bringer of good tidings. Notwithstanding Raven's constant croaking—'He comes. He comes.' Caw. Caw. *Caca! Caca!* Watch where you step in your running. Have your parents not taught you how to behave around the ancients? Don't think you can get by with ignoring me. You owe me an apology. I deserve your recognition and respect. And I'll get it or you'll suffer some consequences, I can assure you. You are in the land of my ancestors. Do you realize that? Remember that? And that's a very old, old land, indeed. Their spirits expect respect from the scrawny-legged likes of you, Huehue Coyote."

Coyote had to focus keenly to see Horned Toad in

the sand. The lizard's tan and gray camouflage was effective. But once seen, Horned Toad looked as bad as he sounded. So Coyote gave a silent prayer of thanks that Horned Toad was only a miniature replica, a reduction of his giant lizard grandfathers. Horned Toad's head was spiked and stickery, as was his back. Tiny little needles stood erect on his round and flattened body. "*Qué feo,*" thought Coyote.

"Oh, Horned Toad, I did not see you there in my pathway. Apologies all around, friend. Your words and voice match your appearance, *viejo.* I just happen to be in a hurry at present. Raven and I race Sun to see the storied Lava rocks of El Coyote."

"*Perfecto,* Coyote, and I'm traveling to Lavaland for a little 'cosmic orgasm,' some 'celestial convergence'—as well as to sleep in my favorite craggy shade out of the way of such yapping interlopers as you. And, yes, Raven announced your coming with his incessant *caca* caws. He is no more welcome here disturbing my solitude than you.

"Look at him up there winging his way into the sunset. About now he's usually diving drunkenly into the River Cottonwoods ready to roost with all his black buddies. They have belched me out of their stinking mouths more than once! I know you guys. You tricksters stick together to be sure. I know what you're thinking. Do not relegate me to the status of a goat-head thorn," sputtered Horned Toad, and blinked his strange bleeding eyes. Eat me at your peril you pathetic peripatetic recidivist."

"Horned Toad, *qué vato, hombre! Cálmate.* I know you are grouchy by nature but this railing of yours is uncalled for. You're going to pop those eyes right out of your *cabeza loca.* Speak of respect! How about the seriousness, the profound purpose which motivates me? Do you think I want to be here listening to you complain and watching your ugly bloody-eyed visage? I must be on my way. Your complaints are something I don't need."

"Well, I've heard it all, now," grumbled Horned Toad. "I didn't hear your howl last night. I noticed the silence like everyone else. And for a change I appreciated not having to listen to your yelps and yaps and barks and that long-held silly sustained howl of yours. Oooooooooooo! Ouch! But you've been losing steam all along. Howl only now and then, if you don't mind. That's my feeling on the matter. Over the past few nights I noticed the waning of your volume and your tone. Raven says you cast the blame on Moon. But you bring some of this on yourself. If you felt a bit more out of sorts yourself, like me, maybe your howl would return to you. Don't you complain when you howl? Complaining has its own pleasures along with its perils, *comprende?*"

"*Basta. Basta,* Horned Toad, *por favor.* This is serious. I'm faced with never howling again. Is that what you really want?"

"*Nunca, vecino. Nunca.* Horned Toad must complain. Coyote must howl. And I admit you often give voice to just how I feel with some of your youthful yearnings. For I too have my more romantic desires. So every once in a while, under the right light of Moon, when the Foothills are bathed with just the right luminous glow, I welcome your serenades. How can I help, *Comacho?*"

"Accept my acknowledgment of your presence and your lineage, your great lizard linkage here in the shadow of this oldest of places. Your blessing and wish for safe passage and success in this trial which faces me is all I can ask."

"Coyote, do you see that largest rock yonder? There at the very base of *La Mesa Negrita?* Take me there, *por allá, Amigo.* Take me there. I want to show you something."

"*A sus órdenes, Señor.* But let us hurry. *Vámonos ahorita,*" said Coyote with visible impatience. "This is the first time you have trusted Coyote so. You know I must carry you in my mouth. And you know of my hunger. Only Mouse has helped me in that most ultimate of ways today. And Cactus tunas."

"Coyote, this is a special time, but not that special. Keep things in perspective. I suggest you carry me on your long nose. That's trust enough for this occasion. Trust is courage. Courage is trust, you know."

So Coyote leaned forward, placing his nose right on the Foothill pebbles and sand, and allowed Horned Toad to climb onto his long nose. Seeing Horned Toad riding there spread out in a kind of comic ownership caused Coyote's eyes to cross and prompted a couple of deep-throated gulps. Then Coyote staggered slowly to the large rock with Horned Toad shouting out the directions with total confidence and aplumb. The large basalt boulder was not all that far and soon Coyote dipped his head and in a long-snouted slide let Horned Toad down to the base of the rock.

"Look here, Coyote. Look at this white image, the drawing on this rock. Is it familiar to you? Do you recognize it out of dream or memory?"

"Well, Horned Toad, my eyes are still somewhat out of focus from watching you at such close range. But I am not blind. The picture looks like you. This is a rock etching of you. If Raven had not told me about such things, I would think that you carved it with your spines, perhaps as some portrait of vanity or in some romantic attempt at capturing essences, truth, beauty. Horned Toad *El pintor. El artista. El poeta.* Is it not one of a kind? A prototypic pattern drawn in respect for you by the ancient Humans when they first visited Lavaland? This is the entrance to Lavaland and this is Horned Toad Rock, is it not? Its full significance I do not fathom. But I seek Coyote Rock somewhere on Black Mesa or on Volcano's rim. I am clearly on the verge of the final revelation, as Raven has explained it."

"Coyote, you are so smart and you are so stupid at the same time. So knowledgeable and so naive in your youth. This is only one such shadowed image of many, many others. This happens to be my favorite likeness. But there are others. The trick is to find the carving which matches your innermost imagined, imaged visage of yourself. That will be *The* Lavarock, your own Coyote Rock. And special feelings will emanate from that rock. You are in the presence of great mysteries here, mysteries of the Earth itself, as well as of your own self-knowledge and definition. But as with every passage, every entrance, there is always a continuation. Each beginning is an ending, and each ending is a beginning. This you will soon learn in your own special way."

"I hear and comprehend what you say. And as I listen, Raven echoes your meanings above. He is impatient to return to River, for dusk is here with us now at this entrance. The day ends and the night begins and Moon will soon be rising over the Mountains beyond the distant River—shining on the Bosque, the Mesa, *El Pueblo,* the City, Black Snake Road,

Foothills, and here on Lavaland, Black Mesa, and the Volcanoes. I must go. I must climb this steep and rock-strewn side of the tabletop and search for my own Lavarock and the story it will unfold about my howl, about Coyote."

"*Àndale, pues.* I bring you here to this appointed place and show you this pictured, shadow version of me, of Horned Toad, and offer these words of encouragement as part of the plan now well under way. Remember, the task is to recognize Coyote Rock when you see it, for you will see many drawings, of something which might be, might look like Coyote. But is it?

"You will know, somehow you will know, when you face the right rock. I have not traveled to the top of Black Mesa. Few have been where you go—to the rim of Big Volcano. But go you must. Much awaits you. You enter now into the domain of Rattlesnake. He is one of the few who know the secrets of these badlands. Take courage, Coyote. Raven will give you further instruction as he departs out of the darkness of day's end.

"There are pictures like this from here to the top of the Boca Negra, and many pieces of pottery, shattered and left in the long ago. Pot sherds. Humans of the past times made these pictures and the pottery. Carvings and scratchings on the rocks. Painting and drawing on the pottery as well. This was in the ancient days, in the long ago, closer to the moments when the Volcanoes were hot and spewing with the life force from Earth's center. Closer to that time. But still far removed. Perhaps things were, ironically, more in balance back in the days of the long ago when these pictures were created, even in the tumultuous times of the Volcanoes' beginning.

"In creation there is chaos—and balance, you know, Coyote. I feel more myself, more in keeping with the who of me, who I was and am and can be, when I view this special image on this special rock, among all the rest. I have my favorite picture of you as well, although I have never seen it. Coyote's image is everywhere and nowhere among these rocks, just as it is on the land. But you infuse most of the images in a strange way. Your spirit, you know. Old garrulous Raven is represented amply too.

"I know you do not make the mistake of thinking that all Humans lived at the same time in the same way and are of the same kind. Generations of Humans come and go in the same way generations of Horned Toads and Coyotes and Ravens do. We change. We remain constant. We appear. We disappear. We reappear.

"After the Humans who scratched and carved our images and those of our ancestors on these rocks came shepherds from far away. They thought the pictures evil and carved the crosses you will see on certain rocks. These crosses are meant to nullify the more ancient carvings. It was this wave of Humans who gave the troubled names of their language to all of these places. Names like "Boca Negra," "Rinconada Canyon," "Piedras Marcadas," "Malpais." For the shepherds this was a "bad country," a badland, the *Badlands.* But it was not so in the beginning, not in its essence, in its original conception and creation. Not for Earth, not for the indigenous ones.

"Other generations, other kinds of Humans came. They tried to make this beautiful, natural place a true badland, a dump site, a waste land. These other Humans, those of these more recent times, came and chipped their names and their initials on these rocks, and the dates of their birth and of their passing through here. See there, over your shoulder. V. Buoay. The second month of 1919. He was someone. He was everyone. Maybe it was a woman. Such names and scratchings are everywhere. And they took high-powered guns and shot at the rocks and at the pictures. Chipping them in yet a more careless, chaotic way. Now some wish to save this place. Others wish to dump even more deadly and killing substances. Good and bad, *Amigo. El malo. El bueno.*

"Many generations. Many changes. These changes and constancies, these transitions of past times extend into our day and will continue into the future as sure as these Lavalands, these hard and still rocks, once flowed over the Foothills toward River.

"But find Rattlesnake. He knows the legends of Lavaland best for he is the keeper of the ancient ways and words of these parts. You will find his picture, although in many disguises, in most of these rock carvings. As Rattlesnake's reptilian cousin, I am designated, bothered but honored, to announce this particular opening of the Boca Negra, this particular storied, pictured portal. And as for me, I am tired and seek to sleep. The darkness of night is fast approaching on the canyon's black mouth and your shiny sable companion, Don Cuervo calls you to offer his own final advice and his last good-byes. Listen for Rattlesnake's voice. Listen for Rattlesnake. Listen for *La culebra!* He will appear when you least expect him, for he especially hunts these rocks and the upper mesa at night.

"*Mira al cielo!* Look! Raven is already flying fast toward us and heads for this very threshold rock to give you final instructions. Go with my song, Coyote, and carry me with you in spirit on your journey, just as you brought me here on your long nose. Carry me with you to the very top of this black-mouthed canyon and all the remaining way across Black Mesa to the rim of the Volcanoes.

"I have never actually traveled there, you know, and have only dreamed of the source of Lavaland and heard of its still motion, its hidden creative powers. The powerful forces still abide there. The life which comes from death and the death which comes from life. Few are kind enough to carry Horned Toad any distance as you did. And I forgive you for stepping on me, unawares. I count you friend, even if you do not always watch where you are running. Keep running, *Mendigo vagabundo. Córrele. Córrele,* with my song:

Coyote comes to Lavaland.
Coyote comes to Lavaland.
Coyote comes running to Lavaland.
Protect his path.
Protect his path.
Shield his paws from the jagged pain.
Shield his feet from sharp rock and broken glass.
Show him Coyote rock.
Show him Coyote rock.
Horned Toad searches the Lavalands with him.
Horned Toad searches the Lavalands with him.
Coyote travel with my ancient reptilian blood.
Travel with this blood which flows from my eyes.
Carry that magic with you, Coyote, *Compadre.*
Coyote travel with my blood's oldest knowing.
Travel with the force of red lava's flowing.
Blood and fire take you up to Volcano's knowing.

Blood and melted rocks hardened,
With their now silent howling.
Travel to your awakened howls, Coyote.
Travel in courage and constancy, Coyote.
Howl your arrival to me, Coyote.
As I listen this night.
On this oldest of rocks.
Howl with the knowing of the ancient times.
Howl with the force of the hot rocks flowing.
Howl with Horned Toad's blood's knowing.
Coyote comes to Lavaland.
Coyote comes to Lavaland.
Córrele, córrele, córrele, Coyote.
Coyote comes to Howl!

Just as Horned Toad was finishing his song Raven flew down with a quick croaking of his voice and a sucking of air. He landed with a plop of cautious command on top of the rock claimed by Horned Toad, but also shared by Raven, for his carved image often appeared throughout the Lavalands as a companion visage. Horned Toad spoke first:

"Cousin Raven. Everywhere all the time. That's my ca . . . . cawing *Cuervo.* Leave it to you to interrupt my song just as I was polishing off another chorus. But it's good to see you, even so. Just like old times. Just like our ancient bookend pictures on the rock in the large corner canyon up ahead. And, yes, here too—the two of us, facing each other and talking. You and Coyote are everywhere and nowhere, I was just saying to our young friend here. We knew you would land here eventually as night settles. We saw you circle over Black Mesa, Raven, and then lost you for a time along the side of the mesa and *las piedras grandes y mar-*

cadas. Your black feathers blend in too well with the dark rocks, especially now at dusk. Brother Turkey Vulture soars here sometimes and your shadow is almost as large as his. And there . . . there, I hear Bullbat now. He's coming to see you, is he not? 'Preent. Preent. Skee'it skee'it.'

"As for me, I'm ready to settle in before the rocks lose all their Sun heat. It is a special time here today, for Coyote carried me over here and did not violate my trust. He made up for his initial rudeness and I am glad. His hunger is now on a higher plane, as you know. He now begins the dangerous run up the side of the escarpment. The dangers increase as we speak, especially as he traverses the Malpais and tries to avoid the Human objects strewn here and there, each with their own peculiar threat. There are also the Power Poles with their hideous hums and cackling pops and cracks which fry my brain even here on the ground. But you have warned him of these, I know, for they are more of your world."

Raven jumped sideways to perch on another rock, one with a flatter top surface. He jerked his head from one side to another and twisted his neck to enable him to look down at Horned Toad and Coyote. He opened his mouth for several seconds and moved his sharp, red tongue. Then he croaked these words slowly:

"There is more than the maddening sounds of these poles to worry about, Horned Toad. The wires will fry me, not just my brain. So I listen to their voices and interpret them carefully when I perch on the high poles. As for Coyote, he has cause to be fearful, but he also has cause to take courage. Lavaland is not the easiest of places to search for one's identity and soul, you know. This howling means much to Coyote as it does to all of us. So, as I said in my earlier messages to you, *Viejo,* Coyote appreciates your help as do I. We must all help Coyote this day if he is to help us in turn." And then, speaking more directly to Coyote, Raven almost squawked, *"Vámonos, hombre. Vámonos. La noche está aquí. Vámonos ahora."*

"Sí. Sí. But I must express my gratitude to Horned Toad. He was initially as grouchy in his words this evening as he is in his looks," responded Coyote. "But we have hit a new understanding, the two of us. I appreciate his advice and counsel. He has just offered me a fine horny-voiced song. And I have been listening keenly to the quality of his Lizard voice, as you advised, in addition to his words, of course. His resonant tones go back a long way. They go back past any time I can remember. There is much that is old as well as wise in his voice. He is not quite as crotchety in his fine Horned Lizard song voice as he is in his Horny Toad conversation and first grumbling greeting. So, friend Horned Toad, be assured that I carry your lizard and toad callings with me and will try to use them in my own singing—soon, I am sure."

Horned Toad shrugged and smiled a wide-mouthed smile, one which seemed to split his head almost in half. Then he blinked his eyes rapidly and opened and closed his thin-lipped mouth several times as if trying to moisten his parched and cottony throat. Raven then turned to Coyote, saying: "*Oye,* you know my evening routine. I now must turn back and head for River and the Bosque. The air is a bit too thick and cold for my liking even now, for I have delayed my going for you. If I could guide you further I would. But I have enlisted Bullbat, my cousin the Nighthawk who sees all and hears with his own singing radar. Listen well . . . ,

Nighthawk comes now . . . , do you hear his beeping and preenting and skee'inting.

"It's a simple matter really, if you keep courage. Just climb through these large boulders and once you reach the top of Black Mesa run fast with the moonlight. The boulders are gigantic, I know, and seem to reach out to roll on you and squash you. They are too heavy to roll, my friend. They have been at rest since the old times. Since the beginning. They will only appear to move, to tumble and to shift and to roll over you. I know such motion in my own dreams. Just run. Run. Keep running. Run for the middle Volcano. It is not the largest one of the five sisters. But it is the blackest and is known as Black Volcano. This is your night's destiny and you should reach it by the middle of the night. Remember, the middle volcano. The middle of the night. Other things will converge there for I have also summoned Moon and Wind. *Buena suerte, compadre Coyotl!* I go now. *Adiós, amigo!*"

Raven scrunched his body low and sprang from the rock, cawing his final song of goodbye along the darkened, lava-sided canyon.

Coyote said farewell to Raven and watched him fly for as long as he could before he became part of the encroaching darkness, which took the appearance of shadowed lava, extending out beyond the Foothills. But Sun extended its last rays all the way across the Valley to the Mountains—bringing back once again the evening pinkness, the watermelon pinkness that now framed, once again, Raven's irridescent blackness. The blackness out of which he came and into which he flew.

Coyote stood surrounded by the chaotic pattern of lava rocks strewn there out of the ancient past, ordered and random, scattered and organized, pushed out on the land from a slit in Earth's surface. A giant, pliant oozing. The dark rocks were cooling and glistening and hardening at day's end. And they loomed large and menacing over Coyote. He stood surrounded by the chaotic pattern and puzzle of the lava rocks still and quiet yet loud and booming out of time's constancy and change. Coyote stood and watched for a long and yearning time as Raven soared to acknowledge Nighthawk, who swooped two or three times in his honor and called out his nocturnal hello. Then Raven flew far down the Foothills, over the moving spots of lights on Black Snake Road. He circled once, and hesitated, looking for carrion, late as it was. Coyote was with him once again. Soaring high with Raven for his Bosque branches. Raven continued on toward the line of golden-leaved trees that defined the Bosque at dusk as it did each dawning. Raven's distant voice blended back upon Lavaland and into the strident staccato preents and beeps of Nighthawk, who now cried out for Coyote to climb the boulder-strewn incline up the escarpment to the head of Boca Negra Canyon and on to the top of Black Mesa.

Be vigilant. Be vigilant. Be vigilant.
Be wise. Be wise. Be wise.
Coyote be vigilant.
Coyote be wise.
Climb Coyote, climb.
Coyote, climb. Climb. Coyote.
Climb high. Climb fast. Coyote.
Before you waits Coyote's imaged self.
Before you waits your own heart's howling.
Before you Coyote. Behind you Coyote.

We soar and sing about Lavaland.
We soar and sing above Lavaland.
We soar and sing over Boca Negra's rocks.
We soar and sing the way to Coyote's rock.
Coyote climb in your coming.
Coyote climb in your going.
Climb, Coyote, climb.
Be vigilant, Coyote, in your climb.
Be wise, Coyote, in your coming.
Coyote comes to Lavaland.
Running, Coyote comes.
Be wise. Be vigilant.
Coyote. Coyote.

Coyote was pleased to hear Nighthawk. He was sad to hear Raven's going, but grateful to Raven for bringing him to Lavaland. Raven had pointed Coyote on Arroyo's path, a new path toward the Volcanoes and not across Arroyo as was usual. This was the ancient path of the lava flows, the path of the several escarpments fingering their way down Arroyo to River, lava flows seeping and crawling out and flowing forward. Before. Behind. Around. Such was lava's coming.

Raven had shown Coyote to the rock portals of Lavaland. And Raven was returning to his River roost with the night's advance. Now Coyote took heart at Nighthawk's song as he climbed higher—his paws now tender and sore from the long day's trip. The sharp-edged lava boulders loomed over him, reflecting their aged, shiny black patina shadows and on them the pictured images in ochre and caliche white of others of Coyote's cousins, animal and Human. All had come this way over the ages, the carved and the carvers, those who had been etched into the rock sides by

Humans who sensed the storied holiness of this place and who added their presence to a landscape at once responsive and abiding. Others had desecrated these rocks, this place, this land brought into a new yet ever so old shape and form.

Behind the blackness of the lava rocks and the shadows which fell around him Sun still blazed orange red in the far west, making Coyote believe for a moment that he was traveling on a journey back to the times when the Volcanoes first spewed forth from the large fissured lips that ran along the horizon and that were his destination. It was, Coyote imagined, something like the magic bleeding of Horned Toad's small eyes, only on a vast, sublime scale.

It took some minutes for Coyote to realize that the ground around him was covered with chips and pieces, particles and slivers of glass—all kinds and colors of glass, white, red, amber, blue. All shades of the four great colors Coyote knew. Colors which informed all the world. Even the lava rocks had been broken and chipped into fragments by objects of tremendous yet relatively puny power. Just what this represented puzzled Coyote until he remembered the booming, echoing sounds and shocks of the guns that had been pointed his way and that his parents had told him about; which he had seen used with deadly and destructive force on flesh and bone.

Coyote, in his climb, was scrambling through a firing range where certain Humans had blindly taken aim, sighted down their barrels and scopes, and shot glass bottles which they set on the rocks. Targets. Blasting away at bottles. Blasting away at the very rocks themselves. Rock sanctuaries and altars. Rock pictures of the sun and the cosmos as fatuous bullseyes. There was glass everywhere and Coyote, in the subdued graying dark dusk, could not avoid cutting his feet. His paw pads bled. Like the flowing red lava out of the earth. Like Horned Toad's magical, magenta bleeding eyes. Like the ravaged and mutilated carrion on Black Snake Road. Like the bodies of countless animals hunted, in religion and in sport. Used and misused. Blasted and abandoned. Killed and consumed for sustenance.

Then he noticed, among the wounded rocks and their carvings, more debris of the Humans—cans and wire, and pieces of old carpet and bedding and old black rubber tires thrown around the base of the rocks—placing them almost in a mood of mourning, or so it seemed to Coyote. Then one large white boulder rose up and scared Coyote as if some spectre threatened to squash him, suffocate him and send him to the spirit world. It was teetering on some rocks just in front of him and it was nightmarish and frightening to the bone. It was . . . , it was . . . an old refrigerator, an electrical appliance as Humans called them, designed and discarded before the days of the giant power poles. This mechanical advancement brought electric current to improve on ice, heat to make cold, but soon obsolete, cast out, thrown away there with all the other trash and discarded objects and detritus.

Coyote was indeed walking through the Malpais—not the badlands of lava mounds and crevices and sharp edges, but the bad country of a Human dump site. The holy rocks had been violated in the most crass and corrupting and uncaring of ways. Coyote regretted that he had to see it this way and that this once wild and primitive and sanctified place, this indigenous sanctuary had become a dumping ground and would stay that way for the longest of times if not forever.

Coyote whimpered out loud, and his sound, although weak, was echoed by the rocks and the lingering ricochets of the bullets that flew into this seasonally sunny appendage of the Black Mesa and its Boca Negra. Coyote whined, and his whine echoed the spewing and flaming lava which at one time gushed in hot, howling force and the great groan of the gas and the lava and its energy which created the invisible shapes and forms made visible in Lavaland in those first times of this place.

It was that force, that power of coming forth, the hot flow and old becoming new which rekindled Coyote's urge to run on and to howl loud and howl hard. He must sing of that force, of its creation and of its corruption and subversion. He must sing of the sacrality and the profanity of what he was walking through. He must sing of that creative moment and of its attempted destruction which now in this immediacy he felt pulsating through him, inside him, grumbling and groaning with sympathetic vibration to the very hunger pains still rumbling through his innards.

He could hear it. He could hear the rumble and the roar and the hiss and the stewing of that original creative moment, creation evidenced around him and now more and more clear and present and loud on his consciousness in the loud rattling which now penetrated his awareness near the top of the great encompassing and surrounding black tabletop, the blackened black Boca Negra of the soon to be reached Black Mesa of black rocks seen in black night in the blackest, soon to be moonlit spaciousness of Lavaland. And there, just as Coyote was about to climb through the last and final boulders of his physically and psychically booby-trapped ascent to the tabletop, just there . . . out of the near and the distant days of Coyote's drifting and dreaming was Rattlesnake. And Rattlesnake was coiled and shaking her tail and she was hissing and singing.

So . . . , so . . . , so . . . , Coyote.
So . . . , so . . . , so . . . , Coyote.
Here you are come, Coyote.
Here you are come, Coyote.
As I go on my evening hunt.
Here you are come, Coyote.
To Lavaland you come.
To Lavaland you come.
Come from Raven's black winging way.
Come with Nighthawk's blunt-nosed diving.
Come from your Bosque home.
Come for your Howl.
Come for your song and its singing.
Come to find Coyote's imaged rock.
Come to visit Rattlesnake.
Come from Coyote's past.
Come from Coyote's future.
Come from Coyote's present.
Come from Coyote's present.
Come to Black Mesa.
Come to Lavaland.
Come to see Rattlesnake at home.
Rattlesnake right at day's end.
Rattlesnake right at night's beginning.
Come to Black Mesa.
Come to Lavaland.
To see Rattlesnake.
To see Rattlesnake.

So . . . , so . . . , so . . . , Coyote.
So . . . , so . . . , so . . . , Coyote.
Here you come.
Here you are.
Hear, hear, hear, hear.
Hear, hear hear me here.
Here, hear.
I rattle, rattle, rattle this arrival song.
I rattle, rattle, rattle this
Here you are, hello.
Closer, closer, Coyote.
Closer, closer, come closer Coyote.
Rattlesnake at, at, at, at your service.
Rattlesnake *a sus órdenes.*
At at at at your service, Coyote.
Rattlesnake *a sus órdenes, a sus órdenesssssssssss*

Coyote was mesmerized by Rattlesnake's song. She was coiled between two large lava boulders, each with her large-headed, lightning bodied, rattler ridged tail carved onto the flat, glistening surfaces. And Coyote's startled surprise now turned into a kind of subservient gaze, with eyes fixed on Rattlesnake and on her companion rock images.

Coyote's eyes were held by Rattlesnake and his ears were captivated by the buzzing, vibrating, oscillating tail. High above, Nighthawk's beeps and preents wafted in the darkening sky as Sun descended behind the Volcanoes and floated down to Coyote consciousness in a syncopated nocturnal sing-song. Only Nighthawk, from his soaring could see the yellow face of Moon rising over the distant mountains, back across Black Snake Road's and River's ribboned way. Coyote's blood chilled in that moment, in the early evening air. And he attempted to shake off the chill of Autumn in accompaniment to Rattlesnake's shadowy subsiding shaking. Finally Nighthawk's noises filtered into Coyote's more alerting awareness.

> Beware Coyote.
> Beware Coyote.
> Be brave Coyote.
> Be brave Coyote.
> Be brave Coyote.
> Beware.
> Be brave.
> Prepare. Prepare.
> Preent. Skee'int.

And suddenly Nighthawk swooped down to shake Coyote out of his confused stupor and forced him to step back out of Rattlesnake's striking distance. He stepped into a clump of Prickly Pear cactus and, thinking he had been bitten by Rattlesnake, he let out a yelp surprisingly loud in its spontaneity. No time for the tasty cactus tunas now which he enjoyed in the day gone by. Pleasure and pain were mixing for Coyote. He knew that under different circumstances he could go in close for Rattlesnake's neck and bite and shake her in half.

"Be off with you, Nighthawk, you old Goatsucker," said Rattlesnake in a curseful hiss, more to herself than the already soaring bird. "Fly after the gnats and bugs and moscas you so drunkenly chase, *pajarito nocturno.* Away with you, batty Bullbat." And Rattlesnake uncoiled a bit, revealing the objects of her concern: her children, who now slithered out and around her as the ancient yet abiding lava had once slithered out from the fissures in Mother Earth.

"Oh, Rattlesnake," rallied Coyote in reply. "I am relieved that you are not angry with me. For I see more clearly the reason for your rattling. You have your brood with you. How many do I count there? Two, no four, five youngsters. I know you search for food this night and that you have found just the proper rock crevice for the coming cold. It is an impressive house, decorated with those images of yourself and your lightning-like ways. Be assured I hunt not for you this night and intend your children no harm. I wish them to thrive long after I have passed this way, for I am only passing through, a sojourner on my way up this canyon's mouth to the tabletop yonder and then on to the Volcanoes, as Raven has instructed. I travel to the top of Black Mesa and on to the five sister volcanoes in search of my howl. I hope to find my imaged and pictured Coyote rock as well.

"Perhaps we share a rock in the same way that Raven does with Horned Toad, or maybe Turtle, or even Parrot. I have seen curious combinations and shapes on this climb. There is hope, says Raven, that here in Lavaland I can regain my howl, find out if Moon took it, or Wind, talk to them more closely. Find out just where my howl is, for perhaps it is still echoing among these rocks like the last echoes of your recent rattling. Like the last reverberations of Volcano's pouring forth. Coyote unable to howl is absurd, you will agree. You must appreciate my anxiety. What would you do if you could not rattle as you so marvelously do tonight? Do you know of my presence among these rocks? Have you heard echoes or seen pictures of me here? Have I wandered here before in a previous life? Is my destiny behind me or before me?"

"Lavaland is a vast place, Coyote, much larger than your imagining. Much vaster, more disturbing and more beautiful than your dreaming. Do not underestimate this terrain, for it is wide and various and vast and new in its very oldness. But of course Rattlesnake has seen Coyote's presence among these rocks and, more than once, impregnated in the very stone itself. But you know you too are seen as both good and bad. So the Human artists thought twice, thought long before they claimed you as either deity or devil and infused themselves with you, claimed or denied you, on these rocks. You know my reputation, do you not? Raven and you and I have these legendary things in common. Yes, I have seen you here and others of your kind. But it is a remote place, and Coyote comes only for special purpose. Ghost or shadow or substance. You are here now and have been here before and will be here again in the mystery of change and constancy.

"I have seen a rock or two with your resemblance carved on its iron surface. This Boca Negra is a vast album, a vast accounting of our times here. And the other canyons of the various escarpment fingers contain many more pictures. Those who went before us are present throughout Lavaland. Searchers. Seekers. Discoverers. I do not think the rocks you seek are at Volcano's rim. They are at the head of this very canyon, just beyond here. Other answers are at Volcano's rim. But I can point you toward a Coyote rock or two. You will choose which one speaks most clearly to you. Which one knows most about this matter of howling. My kin were here when your rocks were imaged. When you were seen and imagined in your coming. My kind came here soon after these rocks cooled from their first heated flowings.

"This is not the question, though, is it? My history. My story. Except as it crosses yours. The question is really one of readiness. Are you worthy to visit this sacred and profane place, to cross it and absorb it in a sustaining way? Can you assure me of your motives if I do point the way? You are known for your . . . , well, for your insincerity, shall I say? Even now you may be figuring out how to kill me and consume my young. What about trust and trickery, Coyote? What about that?"

"I do what I must Rattlesnake. *Como tu.* There is no trickery or fakery involved in this journey, I assure you. Coyote comes here both in fear and in courage, in indecision and in determination. I can only tell you it is better for me and I hope for you and all of our cousins when Coyote howls. And I can't howl at present. I have traveled far this long day and I bring with me the voices and the advice of many whom I have met along the way: Raven, of course, in his directives. He is with me even now in spirit though he returns to his Bosque perch. It was Raven who directed me up Arroyo rather than across it as is my custom. Muskrat, Duck, Quail, Beetle, Mouse (it was his small but strong body that kept me going), Horned Lizard, and Nighthawk, your pesky friend, who seeks only to do his duty by me. Even my friendly adversarial prey, Jackrabbit, wishes me success in this quest. Your old antagonist Roadrunner showed me the way under Black Snake Road.

"Surely if I can pass this way in my crossing of Black Mesa I can pass by Rattlesnake without crossing you. I seek only your direction and your . . . , yes, your all important sanction and sponsorship. Dare I say, your blessing?"

"How is my friend Roadrunner? Still repeating himself? Like you and Jackrabbit we have a love-hate relationship. We reluctantly depend on each other. But do not talk at any length about Black Snake Road. I accept no comparison with it. It is metaphor, friend Coyote. A howler like you must surely comprehend metaphor. It is real. Death resides there. But why must my family name be associated with the evil of Black Snake Road? Such myths are wrongly perpetuated. Black Snake Road is a Human creation and has claimed many of my own kind. Killed more of my family than Roadrunner has ever dreamed of doing. Black Snake Road, as you call it, has deprived Roadrunner and Rattlesnake of many of our more natural contests. This is a big concern with me, Coyote, as you can tell. But it is part of your Lavaland education. Is this place a badlands in and of itself or because it was so perceived by certain Humans who call it so?

"For me it is a good place. It is my place. And, Coyote, do not pretend that you and your kind have not sought to do me in when I have descended from these Lavaland rocks to hunt, and when floods have washed me down to the foothills and mesas below."

"Relax. Relax. Rattlesnake, the shadows of Black Mesa descend and Sun's fire recedes behind the Volcanoes. I must find my pictured self and reach Volcano's rim. Moon is beginning to rise, I see, and now I am near my destination. Rest your many rattles, rattles numerous in honor of your long years here in Lavaland. I leave you to your ways and to the care of your fine children wriggling and waiting about you there. And I hope you will send some of your sound and voice with me. I will remember you, Rattlesnake, and our talk here this early Autumn-advancing evening, the time when the shadows fell and covered Coyote here in Lavaland. Here in *la tierra de la culebra de cascabel. Ayúdame, Señora, por favor."*

Rattlesnake calmed and uncoiled herself further and almost ceased shaking her buzzing tail castanets completely, saying softly in a whisper,

> Coyote go your way.
> Coyote go your way.
> Reach this canyon's dark mouth.
> Reach this canyon's dark mouth.
> As you leave Boca Negra.
> There, there, there is a Coyote rock.
> A Coyote rock is there.
> A Coyote rock is there white in the night.
> White in the night's early moonlight.
> White in the ancient presence of the present.
> Coyote Rock will speak to you.
> Coyote Rock will speak.
> If you listen, listen, listen.
> If you l i s t e n . . . .
> Then to Volcano rim.
> Then to Volcano rim.
> Coyote will howl, he will.
> Coyote will howl, he will.
> Remember Rattlesnake.
> Remember Rattlesnake.
> Rattlerattlerattlerattle.
> Rattttllerwillllisssstennn.
> As you leave Boca Negra.
> As you arrive at Black Mesa.
> Remember Ratttleesnake.
> Remember, yes, yesssssss.

And so Coyote walked past Rattlesnake and her crevice brood, and continued up the black canyon toward its mouth, treading his way still among broken glass where bullets had shattered the silence and the sanctity of Lavaland.

Nighthawk led Coyote further up the Canyon toward the top of Black Mesa. Moon had topped the distant mountains and Coyote turned and looked at the deep yellow moon of late Summer's ending, noting a residual warmth emanating from the rocks and reaching up to Moon who in her fullness radiated out from the Mountains, across the neon-lighted street-lamped city, across Valley and River and Bosque and Foothills and all across the blackness of Lavaland. The Rocks still radiated with the day's heat, now combining with Moon's light to push back Night's chill and Wind's enhancements. It seemed to Coyote that Moon was speaking to him in her soft glow:

"Follow Moon's path to the canyon's head just ahead and then on to Black Volcano's rim, Coyote. Run. Run. Run straight toward your Rock and back into your nocturnal dreams and the silent sounds of Coyote Rock and the echoing volcanic songs of Lavaland. Raven is now back at River, listening, watching, waiting. Duck, too, is waiting in the reedy marsh of the Oxbow. Rush is waiting, whistling softly to itself and to Muskrat and Frog and Turtle. Beetle pauses and rests, listening. Listening. They are listening. Quail dozes in the mesa sage. Waiting. Jackrabbit and Roadrunner are trying to sleep, remembering your encounters. Waiting to see what will happen on the stages of your journey and on your arrival. They are dreaming it. They are imagining it. They are with you even now on your final day's journey. Your cousins send their song with you. Horned Toad and Bluetailed Lizard travel with you. Remember their words. Remember their voices. Rehearse their songs in your mind. Capture their tunes. Their songs. Nighthawk sends out his call to you, Coyote. Run. Run. You are almost there."

Coyote's eyes focused to the moonlit shadows and the growing nocturnal world around him as he trotted further and further up the boulder-strewn canyon where Nighthawk was circling and swooping and diving high in the moonlit sky. The air was clear and cold in Coyote's nostrils. With each breath he inhaled the aromas of summer ripening into autumn. He stopped to mark a large chamisa bush. He heard the insects sing. Cricket and Cicada. And Grasshopper. And he watched and believed he heard Millipede run swift-legged over the sandy path Coyote followed. "Run, run, run, run, run, run, run, run, run, run, run, run, Coyote. Run!"

Night was beautiful and the stars wheeled above him. The shape of the giant cup tipped down and seemed to spill out thousands of twinkling stars which now were reflected in the twinkling lights of the city sprawling beyond River. Coyote looked back again at River and at the Valley where the Humans lived. Some of them had come up to Lavaland from Valley long ago. They had settled there in their westering. They had come down from North country. They had come up from Mexico. It was a geographical node, a focal point which Coyote could feel as he looked out and up at the convergence of lights. Coyote looked back at Black Snake Road, now splotched bright with the lights of their Motion Machines still scurrying back and forth along its course.

The City lights spread out along the Valley. Shining. Shining. Reaching up and out of the ambient City glow to Moon and to Stars. Coyote had never seen such panorama of Nature and Human civilization merging, and he knew he had to live within that convergence for neither was now reversible. Which would win in the struggle for dominion, he did not know. But Coyote would have to contend with both and with the forces behind them both. Coyote would have to find balance between wilderness and civilization, all without forgetting the what and the why of wildness. This he wanted somehow to say in his howling. The complexities of new and old, past and present and future converged for him. The purpose of his journey was beginning to fall into place in new ways. The purpose was congealing. His place within the places set out around him was becoming clear.

The City. Its lights. Far and high on the mountain crest he saw the red lights of television transmitters and microwaves. Up the side of the mountain, there in the crisp night air of Mesa, he saw tiny lights sliding up the side of the mountain, sliding up to the top—and down to the bottom. More Human Motion Machines—but these more serene and slow. Tiny moons, really. Tiny moons.

And just beyond the treeline of the Bosque were the blue neons of a tall building. And more to the right, the green neons of another tall building. Long strands of lights coursed from the Mountains, through the Canyons and across Valley bridges, far, far toward Mesa and the long inclines of the Foothills. And other long ropes of lights reached far up and down River, as far, as far as Coyote's eyes could see!

There, further down the Bosque treeline and across

River on the East Mesa he saw the lights of the airport. And the runways. And above them the lights of airplanes flaring, flaring low, and flaring long, readying for landing like gigantic spirit birds. And above him were birds. Night birds. Nighthawk still, yes. But wing-whistling birds too. Waterbirds. Large ones. Geese. Geese heading to other waterways which he could only intimate.

The lights of the City were many and they were twinkling in the crisp air, reflections of the many stars above. And the glowing planets. And the Big Dipper and the other constellations carried out their nightly motions, imperceptible, but momentous. And there to the north, toward another city, and over other mountains and volcanoes, other Lavalands, were dark clouds and through them ripped bolts of lightning. Jagged bolts of lightning. Giant snakes of lightning. Hot fire kin of Volcano's knowing.

He turned back to look for Nighthawk and was startled into recognition by a gust of wind which whistled around the rocks in front of him. Nighthawk was at the canyon's head. And Coyote walked the last few steps up the steep incline. There, as he topped out over the head of Boca Negra were several pictured rocks—large and small, unified and broken. Balanced and tipped over. Pictures facing him. Pictures askant and skewed. Faces looking up and around and down and several ways at once—etched on two and three sides of the rocks.

One large round face stared out at him with the roundness of Moon. It held a stalk of corn in one hand and a bow and arrow in the other. It was a sign of harvest and of hunting. It was a sign of this particular time of year and Coyote was not afraid. Rather he felt a locking in of convergent forces, cosmic and geological and geographical. Coyote walked slowly now. Very slowly. Near the promontory he could see at the very head of the canyon a rock which he thought bore a resemblance to him. To Coyote.

As he headed for it, now targeted by Nighthawk's radar-like echoes off that very rock, Coyote passed by another rock, surrounded and almost covered by tumbleweeds. It was a dancer. It was a Human dancer with feathers around its head and with its hands at its hips and its feet raised in alternate rhythms. Coyote could hear the distant silent drums now reactivated. Voices giving motion and motive to the form of the rock and the picture on it. Rock figures were all around him. And he knew them. He was where Rattlesnake had told him to be.

Another figure of a Human, this one with both arms raised, palms upturned, jumped out at Coyote. Was it a shout? A warning? A message to turn back? Soon what Coyote heard from the Human figure on the silent and stationary rock now energized with perceived motion was a prayer going heavenward. It was a prayer for moisture. For snow. For rain. Looming over him then was a figure of Deer and of Mountain Lion. Deer was offering himself to Mountain Lion. And Coyote knew their ritual and could hear the voices of hunter and hunted and he remembered Mouse—and Jackrabbit. And he was respectful of the rocks of hunt and harvest and their meaning.

Coyote heard himself offering words of thanksgiving for being there and knowing what he knew.

> Thank you for the hunt.
> Thank you for the harvest.

Thank you for the times leading to them.
Thank you for the growing time.
Thank you for the Rains of Spring.
Thank you for youth and for age.
Thank you for the courage
To prepare and to continue.
Thank you for the taking.
And for the giving.
And for the times of both.
Thank you for the transition
Time between youth and age.
Now and then.
Thank you for the courage to know.
To go and to stay.
Thank you for my coming.
Coyote has come to Lavaland.
And in the coming Coyote knows.
Coyote knows.

Then Coyote noticed Moon's light shining on a large rock just a few yards from the canyon's rim. There—bathed in Moonlight was another Coyote—a companion Coyote, a constant Coyote, a changing Coyote. A shadow self, large and white and ghostly. But it was flat in its rock roundness, and jagged and sharp in outline. Its large orange oxide eyes were holes in the Rock. Its mouth was open and its teeth were needle-like and sharp—lined and long in the ridges and cracks of the rock. From the underside of the figure, shadowed yet glowing in image, hung full teats, large full dugs, at once young and ripe and full of milk . . . yet dry and hanging, wizened and withered from continued, repeated suckling.

Lower down, a large penis rested in a full, rounded bag, a scrotum also seemingly full to the brimming of semen. . . yet depleted, seed ripening and rotten, seed to plant and seed sown.

And the rock figure was positioned in all of its bodied being in a magnificent stance of a hunkering howl. Head thrown back. Haunches bent and bowed. Tail spread out behind, like a cape of brittle, etched fur and surrounded in moonlight. Washed in moonlight. And Moon was reflected off the rock and out of the mouth of the figure and shone through the eyes and the mouth of the carved Coyote. It was Coyote. It was Coyote howling. And Coyote's image was howling at the real Moon suspended in the starry distance overhead . . . and at a round carved moon some inches away from its head. The reality and the illusion merged. The perspective was at once real yet imagined, character in caricature. And the Rock Coyote was much unlike Coyote, yet so much like Coyote that to his mind he and the Rock were indistinguishable. And then Coyote could hear what he was seeing. The imaged Coyote was howling and in its howling it spoke to Coyote.

"Coyote, you have returned to me. To yourself. You have been traveling for a day and forever. You are here for a moment and for eternity. Here. Under moon. Under Stars. Feeling Wind on your stony soft fur. Hearing your whispering loud silent howl. You cry and are silent for me and for others, for sorrow and joy, for loneliness and for companionship and community, in love and in anger. The stirrings in your heart and soul are many and as inexplicable and encompassing as the sky which covers us this night, each night, over and beyond and past all accountings of time.

"You think Moon and Wind have stolen your howl, have conspired together to bring you here with Raven's coaxing caws, with the assistance of your many cousins. Not so. You have come out of your own yearnings. You are here out of the need to know that when you howl it is heard. That it matters. You can hear your howl now in me just as I hear it in you. We howl as one, part of the same fire-forced, blood-driven creative force which made and gave shape to these Lavalands. Here on wind-chilled, night-covered Black Mesa now you can feel the cataclysmic and creative destruction of Black Volcano in this desolation and dormancy. Hear the roaring shifts in Earth's belly. See the fissures, the many mouths opening to the primal ooze. Feel the scorching fire of these cold rocks."

Then Coyote swooned. There in the mergings of sound and silence before him the white-figure flowed out of the rock, taking shape and motion to whisk Coyote onto a strange and endless plain where he was running. And as he moved it moved beneath him. It was whitish and yellow in the moonlight. Rice grass was everywhere and the tiny white seeds were scattering and falling and blowing as if in a howling Winter blizzard on the great Llano Estacado.

Coyote was running faster than he had ever run and yet he was moving his legs ever so slowly and laboriously over the soft-hard surface of the mesa now become the very Moon itself. And Millipede passed Coyote, his long brown body carried aloft by countless legs which started to break off one after the other, causing Millipede to change into a giant, curved and collapsing white shell. First one and then another white, square, meteoric refrigerator dropped like bombs in his path. Their doors bursting open to an outpouring of Human food, rotted meat, molded cheese, torn aluminum containers, decomposing heads of lettuce—all manner of garbage and refuse. Then Coyote tripped, tangled in long Desert Gourd vines suddenly turned into rusty coils of barbed wire, cutting and searing his flesh, marking him, mutilating him as if attacked by a monstrous branding iron.

And then bullets were whistling over his head, kicking up puffs of snowy rock and fragments of hot ice. And darting and dodging an increasing number of snipers he was ballooning up, up, and away—dragged skyward in a giant cupola formed from an old culvert fragment from which he was suspended. Closer and closer came the high voltage wires of the power poles. And then Coyote passed through them in an explosion of arcing electricity and the cupola was ablaze. And now he was soaring higher in the flaming basket. From which he was looking down on himself and his ghostly double, voyeur facing voyeur. And on all of Lavaland. And he could see everything and everywhere he had been. And where he knew he must go. Where Coyote Girl waited for him. East to the big rivered Bosque which he knew as home and further West, past the Volcanoes and over the vast Valley toward Rio Puerco and a giant cone-shaped mountain, many, many times larger than the whitened, gaping, purple Black Volcano which he had finally reached. And he knew. He knew he was destined to be the Slender Roamer who he was, and that his prize was in the process itself. In the going. In the coming along. And he would always be coming along. Forever and a day. And he was talking to

Moon and to himself as Moon. He was of and on and in Moon. He was River. He was Mesa. He was Foot-hills. He was Mountain and Volcano. His hot gaseous breath huffed and puffed skyward and yet was omnidi-rectional, void and emptied into nothingness, of here and there. And yet full, full of everything, of up and of down. And his floating and running were his howling and his thinking was his feeling. Then, then . . . the Human girl and her dog were there on the plain and they were running with Coyote across the Moon and out of the Moon and they were flying, flying across the white, snowy-hot rice grass toward Black Volcano which now glowed white with heat, pulsating, pulsat-ing as if the very heart of Coyote himself. And his red blood pumping, pumping inside him became the red lava, the molten magma coming from the opening lips, the breathing mouth of Earth. And flowing along with the river of fire was an infinitude of fire rocks and the rocks were the pictures carved on them and Raven, Phoenix-like, flew up and out of the fire rocks, his mouth blazing red with a red coal in it, and his feath-ers, his head and body and legs were smoldering black coal. And Jackrabbit stood up, stretching and stretching until he towered in the sky with Raven. And Jackrabbit looked around, his long ears red and flaming with the fire of the rocks, and his ears and drooping tail were tipped and scorched with charcoal and smoke and then he jumped out in front of the flowing fingers of fire, the plain shaking and trembling with his weight and magnitude. And Rattlesnake was swimming through the lava flow, wriggling and sliding through molten balls of thousands of her wriggling and squirming children, all of them dancing and crackling, crackling and slithering in the neon-lit heat on which they moved. And around Rattlesnake's neck was a giant, sharp and polished lava rock and the gasses were bubbling and spewing from it. And inside Rattlesnake Coyote could see Mouse. And he was alive and squeaking, running back and forth, back and forth, and finally escaping, shed and sloughed off with Rattlesnake's skin, transmuted into the gaping road culvert, into waving Rush. And Horned Toad came scowling out of the malleable, molten rocks and his popping eyes were streams of bloody fire, flowing, flowing into the lava. Becoming that lava. And there too was Roadrunner, stepping high and hot and heavy through the lava, his feet smoldering and his eyebrows blistered and burned carmine and burgundy and his tail one long and arcing flame of fire, his comic antics become gargantuan, become somehow the awesome presence of Quetzalcoatl returning from the Valley of Mexico to the Rio Grande Valley and Aztlán. And then the advancing arroyos of hot lava flowed, steaming and hissing down toward the Black Snake Road, covering the motion machines, sending them screeching into mummified, petrified, frozen-hot silence. Onward the lava flowed, over and under the Black Snake Road, melting the corrugated steel culvert into silver liquid, like soldered cinders, pulverizing it into sparks held perpetually aloft, turning and sputtering like a phantom pinwheel of rubies, juggled in masterful pyrotechnic display. The small lava-stuffed arroyos of the Foothills were converging into Big Arroyo, into the sandy highway of Coyote's morning journey and on, on into River which flooded, beyond any banks, wide and slow into and out of the Oxbow which was a lake without limit—totally submerging the ditches and River itself. And there in the reddish brown cauldron of rock and water was Duck, swimming over and around the tip of Coyote's giant penis, the shaft ringed and braceleted with heavy but translucent turquoise, and replicated in the engorged and black-ringed and segmented rushes and reeds, now new and turquoise green, long and abundant among the brown and bending cattails, standing high and erect and shooting forth one long, flowing, continuous ejaculation of cottony semen now become . . . the Bosque itself. Spreading, spreading to line the edges of Marsh and River. Creeping, creeping out and around Muskrat and his muddy-watered home. And Coyote howled down from Moon and up from Lavaland and his swooning, swirling song dispersed across the landscape. Coyote howled with all his memory and anticipation, with all the words and tones and songs and messages of all those he ever knew and ever would know. And his howl was carried by Wind out further West toward Mount Taylor, out further East toward the Sandias and the Manzanos, out North to the Jemez and the caldera of Valle Grande, resonating, reverberating through the Sangre de Cristos and the Pecos and south toward the Mogollons and the Gila. And his howl echoed and bounced and etched itself into the sleep and the dreams of all who could hear. Everywhere. All over. All around. Hoooowlllll. Hoooowwllllll . . . . Hooooowwwlllllll.

The girl tossed fitfully in her bed and she awakened to the distant but close howl. The howl of Coyote. Coming out of the West this night. From over the highway. From the West Mesa. From the Volcanoes. But somehow echoing off the Sandias. Floating in the night air. Floating down the river. When she first arrived she heard him down by the river, almost in the Bosque itself. Then she missed hearing any howling at all for, what . . . , a night, a couple of nights? She rose out of the whiteness of her bed and quickly wrapped herself in a warm terrycloth robe as she ran to the window and looked out on the mesa and the Bosque. The distant mountains framed her view, giving backdrop to the lights of the city, so still and bright and silent in front of her. She listened. "So mysterious," she thought. "It was a coyote. It was the coyote we saw today, I am sure." And she reached down to pat her big red dog who had roused, alert, from the foot of the bed. "He's out there, Rojo, and he's howling. And I think I know what he's saying and I don't. But oh he was beautiful and a bit frightening in his beauty and in his wildness."

And then she heard it. She heard Coyote howl. And she stood, silent at her window. And pensive. Today had been just a respite. The lull before the life storm taking shape around her. The future she faced. Tomorrow was the day. The first of it. The continuing of it. Yes, tomorrow was the day. She was up to it. She could and would have to face it. She would have to go. She would have to find the answer.

"Father understands, I think," she uttered unconsciously almost, under her breath. We had such a lovely day, considering . . . . And Coyote. He was so beautiful. And their gaze had locked for a fraction of a second. She knew it did. And Coyote, he knew what was in her heart and what she faced. Where was he going, up the arroyo that way? With what appeared to be such determination. Grit. Resolve. Courage. You name it. She needed it. Coyote, she hoped, would be with her. She was somehow with him.

Only in the remoteness of her reverie did she hear Raven call out from the near side of the river. From the far front of the City. From the Bosque where, there in the early hours of the morning, he rested.

"CAWWW, CAWW, CAW. Ah, Coyote . . . ."

READINGS

Bierhorst, John. *The Mythology of Mexico and Central America.* New York: William Morrow, 1990.

Burbank, James C. *Vanishing Lobo: The Mexican Wolf of the Southwest.* Boulder: Johnson Books, 1990.

Dobie, J. Frank. *The Voice of the Coyote.* Boston: Little Brown and Co., 1949.

Dove, Mourning. *Coyote Stories.* Lincoln: University of Nebraska Press, 1990.

Frankl, Victor E. *Man's Search for Meaning: An Introduction to Logotherapy.* Boston: Beacon Press, 1992.

Gish, Robert Franklin. *Native American Myths Retold.* Des Moines: Perfection Learning, 1993.

Goodchild, Peter, ed. *Raven Tales: Traditional Stories of Native Peoples.* Chicago: Chicago Review Press, 1991.

Haile, Father Berard. *Navajo Coyote Tales.* Lincoln: University of Nebraska Press, 1984.

Haslam, Gerald. *That Constant Coyote.* Reno: University of Nevada Press, 1990.

Hayes, Joe. *The Day it Snowed Tortillas: Tales from Spanish New Mexico.* Santa Fe: Mariposa Publishing, 1982.

Hyde, Dayton O. *Don Coyote.* New York: Arbor House, 1986.

Krutch, Joseph Wood. *The Voice of the Desert: A Naturalist's Interpretation.* New York: William Sloane Associates, 1966.

Leake, Dorothy Van Dyke, et al. *Desert and Mountain Plants of the Southwest.* Norman: University of Oklahoma Press, 1993.

LeeRue, Leonard. *Sportsman's Guide to Game Animals: A Field Book of North American Species.* New York: Harper & Row, 1968.

Leydet, Francois. *The Coyote: Defiant Songdog of the West.* Norman: University of Oklahoma Press, 1988.

McCarthy, Cormac. *All the Pretty Horses.* New York: Alfred A. Knopf, 1993.

Lopez, Barry Holstrum. *Giving Birth to Thunder Sleeping With His Daughter: Coyote Builds North America.* Kansas City: Sheed Andrews and McMeel, 1977.

Malotki, Ekkehart. *Gullible Coyote Una'ihu: A Bilingual Collection of Hopi Coyote Stories.* Tucson: University of Arizona Press, 1985.

———. *Hopi Coyote Tales.* Lincoln: University of Nebraska Press, 1984.

Schaefer, Jack. *An American Bestiary.* Boston: Houghton Mifflin Co., 1975.

Schueller, Donald G. *Incident at Eagle Ranch.* San Francisco: Sierra Club Books, 1980.

Turner, Frederick, ed. *The Portable North American Indian Reader.* New York: Penguin Books, 1977.

Wood, Charles A. and Kienle, Jurgen. *Volcanoes of North America, United States and Canada.* Cambridge: Cambridge University Press, 1990.